Chigger

a novel

Raymond Bial

with illustrations by Anna Bial

Chigger
Raymond Bial

© 2012
All Rights Reserved.

fiction
softcover edition
ISBN 13   978-1-934894-38-5
ISBN 10   1-934894-38-9
(also available in hardcover)

BOOK DESIGN
EYE. K

ILLUSTRATIONS
Anna Bial

COVER ILLUSTRATION
Anna Bial & Jack Tsai

Printed in the USA.

Published by

MOTES
BOOKS

Louisville, Kentucky

www.MOTESBOOKS.com

Chigger is lovingly dedicated to my mother,
Catherine Louise Jackse Bial (1924-1981), who brought
such joy to my brothers, sister, and me, and left us with so
many fond memories—especially of our idyllic years in a
small town, not unlike the fictional Roscoe, Indiana.

I.

I SUPPOSE SHE WOULD HAVE BEEN CUTE if it weren't for those bangs. Her hair had been unmercifully chopped off an inch and a half above her eyebrows and to the tops of her ears along either side.

"It'd be better to keep a set of ears like that good and hidden," Buzz Phillips whispered to me across the aisle.

I just shrugged, although her ears were near extraordinary. Besides, at Rutherford B. Hayes Grade School we were accustomed to girls wearing their hair in bouncy, ribbon-tied ponytails.

"She's wearin' jeans—to school!" Since he couldn't get a rise out of me, Buzz turned to Gilman Harris, a tall guy with curly orange hair who, along with Toby Lee, was Buzz's best friend.

Gilman had auburn eyes—the same color as his hair and freckles, but with a hint of yellow in them, like you'd see in somebody's favorite pet dog. He nodded soberly. "And look at those patches on the knees!"

No girl in Roscoe, Indiana, wore blue jeans to school, at least not in 1959. Dwight D. Eisenhower, better known as "Ike," as in the campaign slogan "I Like Ike," was still President. Although we'd gotten a taste of the real world through hula hoops and songs like

"The Purple People Eater," and along with our parents we'd suffered through the Edsel goof-up, our town still resided under a canopy of shade trees and convention. At least that's what my dad said.

We rode our bikes everywhere—to the Tastee Freez for ice cream cones, to Pearson's Grocery for jawbreakers, to the Roscoe Cigar Store & Fountain for cherry Cokes, and to Harold's Barber Shop with the liars' bench out front to hear stories about the old days, because local history was more important in Roscoe than current events. We also visited Griswald's Hardware for ball-bearing wheels for our soapbox racers, because we lived just fifty miles south of Indianapolis and to a certain extent our lives revolved around the Indy 500. Above all, the favorite place of everyone—except me—was the Palace Theater where we went to see monster films, which give me bad dreams to this very day.

Our lives didn't extend beyond the city limits—the chicken hatchery at the Co-op elevator on the east side, the Dog 'n' Suds on the west side, the Skyway drive-in (which was strictly off limits to us until we reached the first year of high school) on the south side, and the Sinclair gas station, with the dinosaur on its sign, and the cemetery on the north side. The town was nestled in an island of trees beyond which the land broke jarringly into the blaze of sky and plains.

However, we seldom rode our bikes beyond the edge of town. In Roscoe we knew the safe limits of our own streets, neighborhoods, and living rooms where, on *The Ed Sullivan Show* Elvis was censored from the waist down. Yet we led rich lives, it seemed to me, for we were new and fascinated with the details of everyday life around us. We could stir up adventures in our own small world under the safest and most predictable circumstances.

Then here comes this girl, "not even starting school right," as Buzz put it, and I don't mean just clothes and general physical appearance. Toward the end of April she waltzed into our fifth-grade class as calm as can be. The trees had already leafed out.

"You're about seven months late," Mrs. Simpson told her dryly.

Sitting up straight, the girl folded her hands on her desktop and spoke with a slight twang. "Yes, ma'am."

A big-boned woman, all angles, with a weakness for flower-print dresses, Mrs. Simpson peered at this new student over her pearl-framed glasses, meaning she wanted a fuller answer, that is, an answer with what she often referred to as "substance."

The girl shrugged. Her eyes had this far-off look like she was wishing to be somewhere else. "We just moved here," she said.

"That much is obvious," said Mrs. Simpson, carefully enunciating each word.

What the girl didn't understand was that people didn't just up and move to a different place without a reason. Even then, they planned school, jobs, and personal matters. In fact, people in Roscoe pretty much stayed put. They didn't seem to go anywhere, from one generation to the next. I was kind of a rare bird since our family had come to town just three years ago.

Toby, a large boy whose wardrobe consisted of a wide assortment of multi-striped t-shirts and a single pair of blue jeans, held his nose and whispered in reference to the new girl, "P-U!" However, I couldn't detect much of an odor about her.

Buzz squinted hard like he was trying to see

inside of her and declared, "Something ain't right about her."

Again I didn't say anything to Buzz. My dad was in the Air Force, so we'd moved around a lot without any relation to logic. What's more, I was a Catholic with a Polish name—Luke Zielinski—in a Bible-Belt town of Protestant people with Scotch-Irish and English roots, and a few Germans thrown into the mix. I was such an earnest daydreamer that people called me a poet, which was about the worst thing a boy could be. I also had this annoying soft spot so that, as well as taking care of all my own pets, I spent a lot of my time rescuing baby birds, lost dogs, and stray cats.

Yet like everyone else in the room I couldn't help gawking at the girl. She had a few brown freckles to match her hair, and her eyes were a deep green color, like I'd seen in pictures of the ocean.

Lips pursed, Mrs. Simpson glanced down at the note from the office, which the girl had presented to her. "Your name is…Eddie…Heck?"

"Yes, ma'am."

Mrs. Simpson's eyebrows went up. "What kind of name is 'Heck'?"

The girl shrugged. "I think maybe it's French."

Buzz whispered to me, "She sure looks like she's almost a cuss word."

Mrs. Simpson next asked, "What kind of girl is named 'Eddie'?"

The girl blushed like a peach. "Kinds like me, I guess."

The corners of Mrs. Simpson's mouth bent downward. "'Eddie' must be short for something."

The girl shrugged again.

"Well?"

"Well what?"

"What *is* your full name?"

Buzz twisted around in his seat. He had sandy hair, light blue eyes, and quite a few freckles of his own. Although not anywhere near being the tallest kid in class, which would be me, he considered himself a big shot as well as a self-declared authority on just about every subject in the universe. "We already got an Eddie in this class," he hissed at the girl.

Across the room, offering up a gap-toothed grin, Eddie Ricker pointed to himself by way of illustration.

Her upper lip curling, the girl glared back at Buzz. "So?"

"So…so…one's enough, and he's a boy like he's 'sposed to be!"

"All right," Mrs. Simpson warned Buzz. Then, turning back to the girl, she reminded her, "I was asking you, what's your given name?"

The girl squirmed in her desk; then she looked Mrs. Simpson full in the face. "I ain't sayin'."

Mouths dropped open around the room. Buzz, in particular, was aghast. He sputtered, "You *got* to!"

"Why?"

"Why? Uh, because you're 'sposed to."

She cast a half-lidded look at him. "And who's gonna make me?"

Buzz blustered. "Well, I could."

The girl snorted. "You and what army?"

"I could, but you're just a girl."

She made a monster face at him, like she just might take a bite out of his leg.

"Children!"

Mrs. Simpson tapped her pointer on the edge of the desk, not loudly, but so methodically it was like

Chinese water torture to us. Some of the students clamped hands over their ears.

Obviously, this new girl wasn't about to cooperate with Mrs. Simpson. Our teacher studied her a moment, then she let go a sigh. "I'd say we've wasted more than enough time here. Open your reading books, children. You know the assignment."

While we studied on our own, Mrs. Simpson dug some old faded textbooks with frayed edges out of the closet in the back of the room for the new girl. She called the girl up to her desk and went over our lessons with her, often shaking her head and clucking, "My land, girl, you haven't gotten any further than that? Where on earth have you been going to school?"

Through the rest of the morning we had reading, spelling, math, and civics (including another rant against Communism from Mrs. Simpson, especially about the nerve of those Russians in launching Sputnik before we got a chance to get into outer space). But, as we recited the lessons we absorbed even less than usual this day, because everybody's attention was on the new girl. In Roscoe everybody knew everybody else's business, but this Heck girl was new and unfamiliar, and she already had a secret as deep as her own name.

With summer vacation just a month off, our school days had become languid. We became drowsy on the warm breezes billowing the curtains out like sails, but not this Monday morning. We were all wide-awake and gawking at the new girl. Sorting through her books, trying to find her place in her schoolwork, the new girl ignored the inspection for a while. Then she began to twitch her nose, and not just little reflex movements either. Like a rabbit, she could really move that nose around.

"I don't believe it," said Toby, his mouth hung open so far I could just about see his tonsils.

"It's practically a miracle," remarked Gilman.

Even the girls were amazed by the feat. People began elbowing each other in the back of the room. "Psst! Look at that!"

I thought it was cute. I even had this strange sensation of liking the new girl.

She entertained us so well that no one noticed Mrs. Simpson gliding down the aisle. Stopping next to Buzz's desk, she looked directly down upon him and asked, "Would you like to tell me what's so funny, young man?" He glanced at the new girl who, acting as innocent as can be, had returned to her schoolwork. Not one to squeal, even on a girl, he said, "Nothing."

"Very well. Come with me, Walter Phillips!"

We snickered at her calling him Walter, his given name, instead of Buzz, his real name.

Mrs. Simpson drew a circle the size of a walnut on the blackboard and made Buzz press his own nose to the center of it for a full five minutes.

The class issued a muffled laugh, a blend of relief and nasty glee. Mrs. Simpson cocked an eye in our direction, which is all it ever took, and we promptly shut up.

Looking at Buzz, nose pressed against the blackboard, we had to clamp our mouths shut tight to keep from laughing, and those five minutes were as trying for us as for him. When he had completed his punishment, he went back to his seat with a chalk smudge on the tip of his nose, which caused an explosion of laughter.

His face as red as a Rome apple, Buzz slid back into his seat, ground his teeth and vowed to those seated around him, "I'm gonna get her. I don't care if she's a girl or not. I'm gonna bust *her* nose!"

When at long last the bell rang for lunch and recess, we swept across the varnished floors, prompting Mrs. Simpson to stick her hands on her hips and exclaim, "Good thing the desks are bolted to the floor, or they'd wash out with you!"

Roscoe wasn't exactly a wealthy town so we didn't have much of a playground, just a patch of asphalt enlarged by blocking off each end of a side street east of the school. Every day patrol boys (always eighth graders who considered themselves some kind of elite guard) put special stop signs at each end of the block.

Outside the limestone building, which Toby claimed was over three hundred years old, I sat down with Buzz and the other guys on the stone curbing by the sidewalk, under the light shade of a sycamore tree.

We ate our lunches out of Tarzan and Superman lunch boxes, which were the style that year. Last year Roy Rogers had still been acceptable, but Howdy Doody and Mickey Mouse were strictly for little kids, and no guy would be caught dead with a Dale Evans lunch box, even if he were just delivering it to his little sister. Of course, each year we had to have a new one, shiny and with un-chipped edges. I would have been content with the Davy Crockett lunchbox I'd had in second grade, but Davy Crockett had long since gone out of fashion and he was for little kids anyway. I might as well have walked around school in a coonskin cap.

As he unfolded the waxed paper around his bologna and Velveeta cheese sandwich Buzz asked, "Where'd that girl disappear to anyway?"

"Search me," I said.

"You must've scared her off, Buzz," said Gilman,

chuckling into his egg salad and dill pickle sandwich.

"Naw," Toby insisted. "She eats out of a paper bag. I betcha a million dollars she does."

That would certainly explain her disappearance. Nobody was so poor that he couldn't afford that most basic of school supplies—a lunchbox decorated with a favorite hero.

As they skipped rope some of the girls in our class sang, "I like coffee, I like tea. I like the boys and the boys like me." But the new girl wasn't with them. I looked for Pamela Young, who was my current love, although I'd never mustered the courage to inform her of my deep feelings toward her.

"Wonder what that new girl's eating for lunch?" asked Toby.

"Probably red worms," Gilman speculated. "And grasshoppers."

"Oh, shut up about her," Buzz snapped. "I'm tired of her taking up all the attention."

But with his question Toby had only added to the mystery about the new girl. Why was she so intriguing? Just because she was a stranger to us?

"Come on, let's play kickball," Buzz suggested.

"Don't have time," I said. "The bell's gonna ring any second now."

"Dang! We've wasted our whole lunch hour on her," Buzz said.

We spent most of the time eating, I thought of telling him. This was especially true of Toby who had an appetite to match his size. But as nearly a new kid in school myself, I went out of my way to get along with the guys.

Then, appearing out of nowhere, acting like she was just about the most important person on the continent of North America, the girl strolled right past us and jump-shot a wadded paper bag into the trashcan.

"Told'ya!" cried Toby.

"Hey you!" Buzz called to her.

The girl pointed to herself. "Are you talkin' to me?" It was then that I noticed the soft light in her eyes, as if she were trying to act tough to hide a deep hurt.

Buzz huffed and puffed. "If you wasn't a girl… If you wasn't…I'd…."

She stepped directly in front of him. "You'd do what?"

Buzz's fists closed. "If you wasn't a girl, I'd punch you."

"You mean like this?"

The girl swung so quickly it seemed like it hadn't even happened, but Buzz's nose was sure spouting blood.

Our mouths dropped open. Toby loaned Buzz a snot-crinkled handkerchief. The girl rocked back and forth on her heels. "If you wasn't a boy, I'd've hit you harder."

As usual, Mrs. Simpson arrived on the scene too late to stop the fight, but with plenty of time to punish the culprits. "We don't fight in this school, young lady," she scolded, her face white, her mouth a tight line, as if she couldn't believe that she was speaking these words to a girl. Snagging the new girl's arm, she escorted her into the school, declaring, "This will have to be reported to the principal!"

I breathed a sigh of relief. Unlike other principals I'd known, Mr. Marsh, better known as Marshmallow, was the kind of man whose every gesture asked, "What should I do?" He was about as solid and decisive as a bowl of Jell-O. Later that day, we heard that because she was so new in school, the girl was not paddled. She only received a lecture about acting like a proper young lady and got sent back to class. But Buzz was thoroughly humiliated.

Gilman snickered. "KO'd by a girl!"

"It was a lucky punch," Buzz claimed, very softly.

"You mean, *sucker* punch," Toby snorted.

Acting like typical best friends, Toby and Gilman laughed so hard they had to grab hold of their desk lids to keep from falling out of their seats. "Wait'll I tell my brother, Albert," Toby said, "and everybody else in town that you got beat up by a girl!"

"You better not!" Buzz exclaimed. "And why don't you quit bragging about your dumb brother for once. Albert this and Albert that! Far as I can tell all he can do is eat, like you!" It was true that Toby often talked about his big brother as if he were some kind of hero. Yet we also knew that around Roscoe news spread faster than hay fever pollen on August afternoons.

When it came right down to it, Buzz simply had to accept his defeat, because in Roscoe most everyone believed in fair play. Besides, if he got out of line, as Gilman told him, "That girl might pop you again."

"Oh, shut up!"

Compared to the morning session, the afternoon dragged on. When the final bell eventually rang and we fled the school, Buzz yelled to the girl (from a safe distance down the hall), "Next time I'm gonna have my guard up."

"You better."

"You just wait and see!"

She squinted at him. "I'm ready any time you

are." She took a step in his direction.

Buzz jumped two steps back.

She laughed. "You ain't scared or nothin', are you?"

"'Course not."

"Well, come on, you wanna fight right now?"

Buzz shuffled. Then, drawing a long breath, he turned into a goody-goody. "I would, except you heard Mrs. Simpson. No fighting in this school."

The girl snorted. "Then how 'bout downtown, or at the park? Or the zoo, which is where you belong anyways!"

"We ain't got a zoo here," Toby said, looking kind of puzzled.

Buzz's face got red all over again, especially his nose, which must have been smarting from all the attention it had gotten that day from both the blackboard and the girl's knuckle sandwich. It struck me as curious that this had all started with the girl's twitching nose. Finally, Buzz said, "Fighting is stupid."

That's the only smart thing he's said all day, I thought.

The girl licked her lips. "Well, I can beat the pants off you at *anything*."

His anger rekindling, Buzz yelled, "Oh, yeah?"

Gilman told her, "Why don't you just go back to wherever you came from?"

Buzz sneered, "She probably comes from outer space."

"Why can't you act right?" Toby asked her to her face, although still a safe distance down the hall.

"You can't just have a boy's name," Gilman explained. "I don't care what you say it is, we're not calling you Eddie."

"You don't have to call me nothin'."

Suddenly Buzz lit up. "Chigger!"

"What?" I asked.

"That's what I'm callin' you," he shouted at the new girl. "Chigger. Because you're just a dang bug and you sure get under my skin!"

II.

THE NEXT DAY THE GIRL SHOWED UP at school with a ratty cloth bag of marbles.

Toby rolled his eyes. "Not marbles! Don't she know nothin'?"

First of all, girls did *not* play marbles, just like boys didn't jump rope. Just as important, marbles were out of season in Roscoe. We played marbles in the autumn when we were winding down for more indoor activities during the cold weather. We began and stopped playing marbles and other sports and games just as the birds migrated automatically, without thinking about it. In the spring, as everybody knew, we played kickball.

All morning Buzz and the other guys smirked at the new girl, shaking their heads in total disapproval. At recess, after we'd eaten our sandwiches, Twinkies, and apples, he called over to her, "What a dumbbell. We don't play marbles in the spring."

"She must've *lost* her marbles," said Toby, pointing to his own thick skull.

Gilman laughed. "She belongs on the funny farm."

The girl's face got as red as rhubarb; then she snarled, "Go to hell."

Several mouths dropped open.

Buzz, in particular, seemed to be in a state of shock. He sputtered, "You cursed on school property."

She hitched her thumbs in her jean pockets. "No shit."

"I'm gonna tell!"

"Fuck you."

Not entirely sure what she meant, except that it was something having to do with our private parts, we backed off. Then the bell rang and, for the first time in the history of Rutherford B. Hayes Grade School, a wave of students rushed back into the school building. As she observed our return, Mrs. Simpson fanned herself with her grade book and declared, "I'd better sit myself down. What on earth is going on here?"

Buzz raised his hand.

Mrs. Simpson said, "Now I know I'm dreaming. I've never known Walter Phillips to volunteer for anything."

Rising from his desk, Buzz stood at attention in the aisle. "Chigger said a bad word."

"Who?"

"Her!" He flagged his arm in disgust toward the new girl. "We call her Chigger on account of her name being so stupid."

The new girl furiously twisted around in her seat. "My name ain't stupid!"

"Is too!"

"Is not!"

"All right now. Let's just drop it, shall we?" ordered Mrs. Simpson.

The girl muttered under her breath, "My name ain't stupid, leastways not as stupid as Walter."

"My name isn't Walter. It's Buzz. And she did say a bad word, Mrs. Simpson! She did! A whole bunch of 'em."

Never in my three years in Roscoe had I thought Buzz Phillips of all people would be a tattletale, which was about the worst crime we could commit at our age.

Mrs. Simpson sighed. "All right, Buzz, just what did she say?"

He looked down at his feet. "I can't say it, not out loud."

"Well, how'm I going to know what she said, then?"

Buzz shrugged.

Mrs. Simpson stuck her hands on her hips. "Why don't you come up here and write it on a slip of paper." She didn't appear the least interested in the matter (even our teachers despised tattletales) until she read what Buzz had scratched out on the notepad on her desk. Angrily, she turned to Chigger. "I ought to wash your mouth out with soap, young lady!"

The girl just sat there, neither snotty nor humble.

Buzz glanced earnestly at Mrs. Simpson. "I ain't sure I spelled that one word right. I—"

"That will do, Buzz!"

Snatching the slip of paper away from him, she tore it into a hundred little pieces, which she fluttered in the wastebasket. Then, hooking her finger at Chigger, she commanded, "Come with me, young lady! To the office! This will have to be reported to the principal!"

Nose in the air, Buzz returned to his seat as Mrs. Simpson escorted the new girl from the classroom.

"You sure showed her," said Toby, punching him on the arm.

Gilman snickered, "Hasn't been here two whole days yet and she's already been to the principal *twice!*"

"Maybe it'll be a daily habit—like saying the Pledge of Allegiance," added Toby, his piggish eyes sparkling in his plump face.

They laughed in the back of the room until Pamela Young turned around in her seat. Her shiny hair in a ponytail and her blouse freshly pressed (even the puffy sleeves), she declared, "You're a snitch, Buzz Phillips!"

"But she—"

"Squealer!" exclaimed John Fowler.

"Canary!" whispered Eddie Ricker, prompting several guys to whistle like the yellow bird.

Buzz reared up in his seat. "But she…."

"Tattletale, tattletale, stick your head in ginger ale," sang Pamela.

They squabbled for a while, then instantly the room went quiet as the door opened and Chigger and Mrs. Simpson returned from the principal's office. Judging from the dark look on our teacher's face, it was a good thing she found us pretending to be at work.

Chigger eased into her seat, which perked up Toby. "She got paddled!"

Buzz, Gilman, and Toby barely managed to squelch their laughter. I frowned. Unfortunately, Marshmallow's being a weakling also meant he easily caved in to outraged teachers.

Lacing her fingers on the desktop, Mrs. Simpson lectured, "Now Chig—I mean, our new student—comes from a big city." She paused to let the words sink in. To us, "big city" meant corruption and bad living in general. "She doesn't realize that there are some things we do differently around here. For instance, children here are courteous and well mannered. But that's all been settled, hasn't it, young lady?" Chigger stared ahead at the blackboard as if she was trying to burn a hole right through it. "Now let's all get back to work. We have lots of ground to cover before the end of school and we can't afford to waste any more time."

The matter might have been settled then and there, except for Buzz Phillips who, by nature, couldn't leave anything alone. Toward the end of the school day he poked Toby and Gilman to make sure he had an audience. I caught on to what he was doing just as he was crawling up the aisle. He loosened the string on Chigger's bag of marbles, which was hanging on the back of her seat, and managed to slip back into his own seat just as marbles splattered all over the floor—cat's eyes, aggies, and steelies.

Mrs. Simpson jumped right out of her seat. "What on earth!"

"They're hers!" cried Toby, pointing to Chigger. "We told her not to bring them to school."

Buzz whispered, "Here we go to Marshmallow again."

Chigger scrambled around the floor picking up marbles, some of us helping her, but what worried me was Mrs. Simpson. She was standing there as tall as the Warner Building downtown, tapping her foot, not for a moment taking her smoking blue eyes off Chigger.

The next afternoon toward the end of recess, Buzz was at it again. Stepping in front of Chigger, who as far as I could tell was trying to mind her own business, he chided her, "I'm glad you learned your lesson about having a dirty mouth."

"Go to hell."

Buzz was livid. "I'm…I'm…I'm…."

Chigger squinted up at him. "Go ahead and squeal. See if I goddamn care."

"Hey, what did Mrs. Simpson and Mr. Marsh tell you about saying those dirty words!"

She just looked at him like he was the most pitiful creature on earth.

"Well, this sure is something your dad should know about," he said, swelling with indignation.

Chigger shrugged. "Well, go ahead and tell him, if you can find him."

"Say what?" asked Toby, his jaw hanging open. "Where is he, anyways?"

"None of your big-nosed business."

Gilman asked, "You mean he don't live at your house?"

"'Course not," said Chigger, making it out to be the most normal thing in the world. Then, head raised, she strolled on into the school like she was just about the most important person this side of the Wabash River.

Stepping forward into the bunch of us, her eyes bright, Pamela Young said, "Her parents are *dee*-vorced." It may have been the first time in her life the word had actually crossed Pamela's sweet and innocent lips. "My mom told me so."

Buzz sighed in exasperation. "Well, how come you didn't tell us about it before?"

"Because you're such an old busybody, Buzz Phillips!" Pamela snapped. She had this way of telling people off that just about melted my heart.

The only other time I'd heard "divorce" mentioned out loud was on *As the World Turns*, which Mom watched as she ironed her way through bushel baskets of damp clothes. Everybody on those TV soap operas was either divorced or getting ready to be. "Just shameful," clucked

Mom as she steered the iron over a shirt and leaned forward for a closer look at the screen. During these steamy episodes she sent me and my brothers, Henry, Will, and Greg, along with my sister, Katie, whom we just called Sis, into the other room, which was all right with me because I despised those dreary soap operas.

Now, Chigger's fighting and cussing could be dismissed as bad habits, but in Roscoe, to come from a broken home was considered just about outrageous. People here were either happily married or, if stuck in bad marriages, they were jealous of those who'd had the good sense to get out of theirs, which made them all the more determined that everybody else should stay married. At least that's what Mom said, and it almost made sense to me. More importantly, I wondered if Chigger's parents being divorced had anything to do with her sudden appearance in our little town.

Later that afternoon Chigger didn't exactly distract attention from the scandal of her broken home when, during a geography lesson about Alaska, she said casually as can be, "My dad caught a polar bear once't."

Buzz blinked twice, rapidly, then, sagging in his desk, he groaned, "Aw, come on. There ain't no polar bears around here. Not a single one."

Chigger contentedly folded her arms like she really had him. "There are in Alaska."

"Alaska?"

"You heard me. What do you think we been talking about here, or've you been sleeping through the school day like usual?"

Toby gawked at her as though trying to convince himself that Alaska was a real place. "Alaska's t'other side of the world, practically."

"It just became our forty-ninth state," Chigger

reminded him as though she were an authority on geography. "It's part of America, even though it ain't hooked onto it like the other states is."

Buzz shook his head. "Your dad ain't never been to Alaska."

Chigger sat up sharply. "Has too! He's lived with Eskimos! He's eaten whale meat! He's been to the North Pole!"

When we had been stationed in Tacoma, Washington, Dad had flown missions to Alaska, so I knew a little about it. He'd brought home king crabs and would have gotten a polar bear hide to be tanned into a rug, except that they were temporarily preserved in urine, so I knew the polar bear story could be true. Unlike the other guys, I knew that there were many other places in the world besides Roscoe, Indiana. I found myself staring back at Chigger. I was on the verge of believing her until she took another deep breath and pronounced matter-of-factly, "'Course he was livin' in Africa last year and Australia before that."

"Aw, come on!" Buzz groaned.

"And next year he just might go on to South America. You never can tell. You ever been to South America, Buzz? It's where they got fish that eat people alive!"

"What?"

"They eat people, 'specially scrawny ones like you!"

Like us, Mrs. Simpson was left speechless for a moment, but the hard edge crept back into her voice when she reminded Chigger, "You know, dear, we mustn't exaggerate."

"Talk about whoppers!" Toby exclaimed. "Liar, liar, pants on fire! Nose as long as a telephone wire!"

"I'm not!" Chigger insisted. "Cross my heart and hope to die. Stick a needle in my eye!"

Buzz folded his arms. "It ain't right to make up stories."

"I'm not. My dad's a geologist."

"A what?" Buzz asked.

"A geologist. He works for a *big* oil company and gets to travel all over the world. Sometime he's gonna take me with him, but right now he sends me all kinds of presents and stuff."

Suddenly, I realized that for all we knew she *was* telling the truth, since none of us were quite sure what a geologist was. Fast as could be, I dug the dictionary out of my desk and looked up the word. "He studies rocks!" I shouted; then glanced back down at the page. "I think…."

"That's right," said Chigger, folding her arms and sagging in her seat.

We all gazed upon her in awe, even Mrs. Simpson.

Thereafter—for about a day and a half—Chigger became truly exotic in the fifth grade at Rutherford B. Hayes Grade School. She was even almost liked, except that her parents were still divorced. At least that's what Buzz said his mom said, and she owned and operated the Curly Cue Beauty Parlor, so she ought to know. However, I still tended to disbelieve Chigger's stories about her dad. She made him out to be such a great guy that I suspected he just couldn't be all she cooked him up to be.

Plus, we soon realized that Chigger had yet another problem. She had spent so much time fighting, cussing, and bragging those first few days that we didn't notice how wiggly she was until well into May.

"She's got some kind of problem, makes her so squirmy that she can't sit still for more'n two seconds," Toby told us one day on the playground. "And you know what else? My mom says her mom works in the shirt factory."

"The shirt factory?" I asked, surprised.

"Well, is her dad a...a...whatever that was?" asked Buzz.

Gilman shook his head. "I doubt it. That's just another cock-and-bull story. That's what my dad says. If he was, then why's her mom working on the assembly line—for peanuts?"

I blurted, "Well, he could be a geologist. You don't know for sure."

Everybody just looked at me.

From the start I hadn't believed Chigger either. But I suspected that she was caught between what she and her mother were leaving behind, whatever that was, and what they were running into in Roscoe. On the way back into school Pamela inventoried Chigger's personal qualities. "She fights like a stupid boy, she cusses like a convict, and she lies like a dog."

"Plus she's always running on overdrive," Buzz added.

I shrugged. "Well, she's not all bad."

Buzz's mouth dropped open. "Huh?"

I explained, "She just needs to slow herself down a little."

Gilman laughed. "I'd just as soon see her keep on running—right out of town."

"Yeah, like Speedy Gonzalez," Toby said. "*Ándale, ándale!*"

As they drifted away from me, Pamela asked, "What's the matter with you anyway, Luke?"

Gallantly I said, "I don't think we should make fun of Chigger just because she's weird and stupid."

Turning slightly away from me, Pamela said, "Or maybe you like her."

"Uh, not really, I just…." Before I could get the words completely out, Pamela, my one true love (at least on an imaginary level), walked back into the school and out of my life.

If Chigger had had any chance of being accepted, it was lost when she lied about her father, because people in Roscoe prided themselves on being authentic, if only because they had nothing else. The next day during recess Buzz was telling jokes when suddenly he turned to her and declared, "Monkey, monkey, bottle of pop, on which monkey do we stop? One, two, three, out goes she!"

"Back to outer space, or wherever you came from!" suggested Toby.

"Yeah!" Buzz cried. "Get her a one-way ticket back to Mars. Just so she gets out of our school and out of our town!"

Chigger glared at him. "Dog shit, you're it!"

Instantly Buzz got red-faced. He stammered, "Uh, that's dumb."

"Sounded pretty good to me," said Gilman, nodding to Toby.

"Yeah, I ain't never heard that one before," Toby agreed, his head bobbing.

Buzz exclaimed, "Oh, shut up! You guys are sure a big help! We're 'sposed to be buddies! We're 'sposed to stick together!"

Gilman and Toby looked at each other as innocently as hound dogs.

Chigger taunted Buzz, "You think you can do

any better jokes?"

"No sweat."

"Well?"

"Well…uh…I ain't got time now."

"Well, I do! And I can do anything better than you can any day of the week. How 'bout this? I see London, I see France. I see Buzz's underpants. They ain't black, they ain't white. Oh, my God, they're dynamite!"

Everyone laughed, except Buzz, of course. "Why don't you just shut up?" he suggested.

"I don't shut up, I grow up! But when I see you, I throw up!"

I had to admit the girl had a knack.

Gilman and Toby chanted, "Come on, show her, Buzz." Toby suggested, "We'll have a contest to see who can come up with the best jokes. Come on, you go first!"

His face becoming as white as skim milk, Buzz just stood there. Chigger told him, "God made mountains, God made lakes, God made you, but we all make mistakes!"

Buzz glanced around for help, but all the guys were looking at their feet or at the sky. Finally Gilman peered deeply at Chigger and asked, "Where'd you come from anyway?"

Chigger cocked an eye at him. "I seen places that'd make your skin crawl."

"Aw, quit bragging," Toby groaned. "We just want to know where you come from."

"The big city," she said.

"Terre Haute?" asked Gilman.

The girl snorted. "You call that a big city?"

"Evansville? Toby tried.

The girl smirked.

Buzz looked at Gilman and Toby in total exasperation.

"Indianapolis," said Chigger importantly.

That meant nothing to us, except for the Indy 500 and all the criminal activity that was said to go on up there—and White Castle hamburgers, of course. Mom detested them, but whenever we visited the big city, my dad, brothers, sister, and I all devoured piles of the little burgers infused with onions.

Splitting off from us, Chigger ran into the school, singing, "Jingle bells, Batman smells, Robin laid an egg. Batmobile lost a wheel, and Joker broke his leg!"

"What a screwball," Buzz muttered, short of breath, looking as though he'd been struck by lightning.

Toby grinned. "I think she likes you."

Buzz thrashed as though awaking from the throes of a horrible nightmare. "Don't make me sick!"

"Buzz's got a girlfriend," teased Gilman.

Toby joined in and they chanted in unison as Buzz threatened both of their lives and chased them around the playground. However, I figured that Chigger must like him and he would probably end up liking her. That was how those things usually worked out.

III.

On Monday I broke a shoelace just as the bell rang, so I came in from noon recess behind the rest of the class. Alone in the hall, I'd stopped at the water fountain for a drink when all of a sudden I heard, "Psst!"

I glanced at the water fountain, perplexed.

"Psst!"

I glanced up and down the hallway of wavy, varnished hardwood floors; then Chigger's head popped around the corner. "You're cute," she whispered, cupping her hands around her mouth, and ran into the girls' restroom.

Instantly I felt sick to my stomach.

For the life of me I couldn't understand why anyone, especially this girl, would have a crush on me. I'd always considered myself the most uninteresting kid in the school. Plus I knew that I shouldn't have anything to do with Chigger, not if I valued my place in the social order of our fifth-grade class.

Relieved that no one had seen us, I went on into our classroom. Immediately Buzz pointed to me and shouted, "There he is, Mrs. Simpson!"

Our teacher stuck her hands on her hips. "We were wondering where you'd disappeared to, Luke."

"Probably out there kissing Chigger!" Gilman teased, puckering up like a chimp, his lips peeled nearly inside out.

Feeling my face redden, I shrugged and said, "I broke a shoelace out on the playground. I had to stop and tie a knot in it."

Two seconds later Chigger strolled into the room.

Mrs. Simpson frowned. "And where were you, young lady?"

Chigger looked surprised that anyone would give a hoot where she had been. She said, "I was taking a pi—I mean, uh, I was in the toilet."

The color rose in Mrs. Simpson's face. "You mean 'restroom,' don't you?"

Chigger shrugged. "Yeah, I 'spose so."

"Very well then. Take your seat, young lady. We don't have all afternoon. We can discuss this matter after school." Mrs. Simpson was the color of a well-ripened tomato. Not for a moment taking her eyes off Chigger, she said, "Pamela, would you like to come to the board and do the first problem?"

Rising from her desk, Pamela made a polite little curtsy in her fluffed-out skirt and said, "Yes, ma'am."

While she worked out her problem on the blackboard, Buzz whispered to me, "You know, that girl ain't got a friend in the world. Nobody in the whole school likes her." Along with Gilman and Toby, he looked hard at me. "Unless you do!"

Just thinking of the incident by the water fountain made me squirm as if a furry, long-legged spider had crawled down the back of my neck.

"Well, do ya?" Buzz demanded.

I swallowed.

I hadn't decided yet whether I liked Chigger or not. I sure didn't think much of her bragging, especially if she was saying things that weren't true. I also didn't like her cussing and fighting. But I didn't dislike her, either, and sure as heck wasn't going to be strong-armed by Buzz Phillips into saying anything either way. As much as I wanted to get along, I wasn't going to be one of his toadies, like Toby and Gilman were. The fact is, Chigger reminded me of a young woodpecker I'd found last year, its right wing all crumpled up. Although the bird was badly hurt, it kept pecking at me, not because it was mean, but because it was afraid, even of being helped.

Before I could explain myself to the guys, Mrs. Simpson asked, "Buzz, would you do the next problem? Come to the board, please."

Buzz sagged in his chair, muttering to himself, "Oh, no."

While he went up to the board, dragging his feet, failed to solve the problem, and got chewed out by Mrs. Simpson for not doing his homework, I thought about how tough it is to be the new kid in school.

Three years ago, my dad had been transferred to Baxter Air Force Base over in Oglesby, but he couldn't find a home for us near the base. So we had rented the white clapboard house with the screened-in front porch on Milford Boulevard here in Roscoe. Although Dad had to drive twenty miles to work every day, it was great to be out from under the shadow of the military base, to be regular Americans in an average town in the middle of the Midwest. This was our fourth move in my lifetime. We'd last lived in Tacoma and, although I'd liked everywhere we'd lived, Roscoe was the kind of place I wanted to be part of for a long time.

I still had scary dreams, which had started when my dad got called up in the Korean War. The whole nation was in the grip of the Cold War, as Edward R. Murrow called it on television, and taking it to heart, I sometimes awoke in the middle of the night certain that we were under attack. One night, just after we'd moved to Roscoe, I'd been so scared that I'd crept down the stairs to the living room.

"What's the matter?" Dad had asked when he saw me standing by the newel post, at the edge of the light.

I rubbed my eyes. "I dreamed that the Japanese were bombing us."

"We're not at war with the Japanese," he said softly.

"I know."

For a moment we looked at each other, aware that even if I was wrong about the Japanese, we might be at war with someone at any moment. It might be the Russians or the Chinese, but we had actually fought the Japanese not so long ago, and I knew that dreams sometimes made more sense than reality.

Having seen a lot of action in World War II and Korea, Dad had learned more than he'd ever wanted to know about war, at least that's what he told us. In her sewing box Mom kept his medals and the pieces of shrapnel that had been dug out of his forehead and chest when he was flying bombers during World War II. My brothers and sister and I often handled them, and I wondered exactly how he'd come by them. Mom only told us, "Your father doesn't like to talk about war because it brings back bad memories." Sometimes he'd mutter something like, "All those people who glorify war haven't ever been in one." He never let us view war movies at the Palace or have any soldier toys.

My father had seen the death and destruction of

two wars up close, and he couldn't make sense of it. So how was I, both in my dreams and in real life, supposed to make any sense of friends or enemies? Hadn't the Russians and Chinese just been our allies? Now, just like that, they were our enemies, and at any time Dad could be called up again, like he had been in Korea. All I knew was that the world outside Roscoe was a very dangerous place, and I appreciated our town for its peace.

I liked Roscoe so well that I made a special effort to get along with everybody. I was what Mrs. Simpson called a model student—quiet, well mannered, and studious. People sometimes called me "Professor," which I didn't mind at all. But I sure didn't like being called a poet, which they also called me because I felt things so deeply. I always had the dictionary by my side to look up the meanings of words and was reading my way *A* to *Z* through the set of *Encyclopedia Americana* in our living room.

I had gotten to be good friends with Buzz, whose father was one of the three doctors in town, and pretty important. My brothers, Sis, and I regularly went to him for checkups and polio shots. I felt comfortable in his office, with its oak trim and old furniture in the waiting room. Although his dad was nicknamed Sleepy, because of his slow-paced manner, he was a good doctor who, when necessary, also made house calls. His father's position automatically gave Buzz a special place in Roscoe, although because he was short he seemed to need to constantly battle to remain top dog.

Gilman's dad owned the hardware store, and Toby's dad was a fireman, so they were considered respectable too, though not as much as Buzz and me, since my dad was an Air Force officer. Toby seemed to have some sort of complex about his weight, and

Gilman was on the clumsy side, but these were small faults.

Chigger, on the other hand, was having a lot tougher time than I'd ever had. In fact, she seemed to be fighting her own kind of war in this town, which I'd always considered so safe. Again I was thinking about the lines between friends and enemies. They were drawn as clearly in our grade school classroom as they were among powerful nations. I couldn't help thinking that the lines didn't make sense. There was no need for us to be always choosing sides, like they did in wars, which never had a happy ending no matter who supposedly won.

As the bell rang ending school that day, Chigger bolted for the door, prompting Mrs. Simpson to call after her, "Don't forget, young lady. I want to speak with you."

"What for?" asked Chigger.

I was sure she wasn't being smart-mouthed, at least not intentionally, but she wasn't exactly being polite either, and I could see Mrs. Simpson puff up like an old hen fluffing up its feathers. She said, "Don't question me, young lady! Just get over here. This instant!"

The rest of us drifted toward the door slowly so that we could see what was going to happen to Chigger. Buzz, Toby, and Gilman were already slugging each other on the arms and whispering among themselves.

"Off to old Marshmallow again?" predicted Gilman, a mean light in his eyes.

"Naw, she's being kept after school now!" snickered Toby.

"Serves her right," said Buzz.

Not paying them any mind, Mrs. Simpson told Chigger, "You were late coming in from recess. I'd like for you to knock erasers out on the back steps, and when you're done you can wipe down the blackboards."

Chigger said, "I done already told you I was in the, uh, the restroom."

"That doesn't matter," Mrs. Simpson said. "You should have asked permission. Maybe next time you won't dawdle."

Usually we loved helping after school, except when it was meant as a punishment. Especially now with the nice spring weather, we couldn't wait to be outside.

Without a word Chigger gathered an armload of erasers.

Buzz called, "See you later, Chigger! We're all going outside and we're gonna be having fun!"

But to me it didn't seem fair. Chigger wasn't that late, just a few seconds after me, and even if she had been late she had an excuse. By rights our teacher should have punished me, too. I hung behind the other guys, wanting to say something to Mrs. Simpson, even though I was usually too scared to speak up to people, especially adults.

Buzz and the other guys called, "Come on, Luke!"

"Hurry up!"

"Get a move on it!"

Guiltily, I turned my back on Chigger, her arms loaded with erasers, and I knew at that moment that, for all my good behavior, I was an absolute coward—me, the son of a war hero.

Summer vacation was just two weeks away, so close that I tingled all over and wanted to think of little else, including Chigger. I figured we would end the school year and she'd vanish for the summer, maybe not even be around next August. However, for the rest of that week, scarcely fazed by having had to stay after school, she seemed to be everywhere—springing out from behind the coat rack, peeking around the sycamore tree, under the fire escape tube, always with the same line: "Psst...You're cute!"

In every instance I just stared back at her, not knowing what to say or do. Things were complicated enough by her cursing, fighting, and bragging. Now she had a crush on me, of all people, and I hardly even liked girls, except maybe Pamela.

Friday afternoon when I got home from school, Mom called from the living room, "Luke, is that you?"

Thinking I was about to be given some despicable after-school chore, I froze in mid-step and reluctantly confessed, "Yes, it's me."

"Come here, will you?"

I eased into the doorway.

With a sprinkler head inserted in a pop bottle, Mom was dampening down the laundry for her weekly ironing. She was a big-boned woman, which was good, Dad always said, considering the loads of laundry she had to lug around the house. She favored plain cotton dresses in pastel colors—none of those gigantic flower-prints like Mrs. Simpson wore. Everything about her was always fresh, clean, and practical, just like the house itself. "Dust doesn't stand a chance around her," Dad often said.

She put down the pop bottle and turned to me. "I hear there's a new girl in your class."

I shuffled. "Yeah, sort of."

"What do you mean 'sort of'?"

"Well, she's new all right, but I'm not sure whether she's a girl or what."

"How come you haven't mentioned her at

dinner?"

I shrugged. "She's not exactly a good topic of conversation, especially when people are trying to eat."

"The way I hear it, she's been raising quite a ruckus at school."

"Well, she hasn't really gotten off to a good start."

Henry strolled in from the kitchen with a double-decker ham salad and potato chip sandwich, one of his favorite after-school snacks. His crew cut stiffened with Butch wax so that it was permanently vertical, three eighths of an inch high, he smirked at me. "Luke probably feels sorry for her. He probably even likes her!" A mechanical wizard and a real nuisance, he thought he was a big shot because he was an eighth grader and about to advance to Roscoe High School. "You know how Luke always has those dopey ideas about saving the world. His heart's as soft as his head."

"Dry up," I muttered back at him.

In preparation for his attack upon me, he sucked in his cheeks and pursed his lips; hence his nickname "Fish Face."

"Keep that up and you'll go cross-eyed," I told him.

"Why you...."

Out of principle he slugged me on the arm, right before Mom said, "Cut it out, boys."

"But he...."

"Don't be a baby," said Mom.

Rubbing my upper arm, I could tell from the set expression on Mom's face that she didn't want to hear another word about it.

With a big, triumphant grin spread across his face, Henry ambled on into the dining room with his high-rise snack.

"I was asking about that girl," Mom said, catching my attention. "The way I hear it she's got a mouth on her like a sailor and she's always tormenting that nice little Phillips boy."

I couldn't say much for Chigger's vocabulary, but I did try to explain, "I think it's mostly the other way around. Buzz is always bugging her."

Mom waved me off. "Don't be silly. I've known his mother since we moved here and you know as well as I do that Buzz Phillips is a perfect gentleman."

"Buzz?" Although Mom and Mrs. Phillips were best friends, I was obliged to inform her, "He gets in more trouble than the rest of us guys put together."

"That's not what I meant. Boys will be boys, of course, but he's well-mannered when he's supposed to be."

"But he and Toby and Gilman have been the ones picking on *her*."

"Well, she probably deserves it. Imagine, a girl fighting right out in public. I hear she's been in trouble since day one."

"But it hasn't been her fault exactly."

"What do you mean?"

"I think she just doesn't know how to act in public. It's like she hasn't been around people much, at least normal ones."

Mom jabbed a finger at me. "Well, you steer clear of her, you hear? I've got enough trouble with you kids as it is without having you get mixed up with some little delinquent."

"Yes, ma'am," I said, studying my feet, wondering what a "delinquent" was, and remembering the siege of "Psst….You're cute" remarks.

Actually, trouble was just about the last thing Henry, Will, Greg, Sis and I ever gave Mom. We were scrubbed until our skin shone. Our hair was always perfectly trimmed—very short in the winter and, with the standard GI haircut we had to get every May, practically nonexistent for us boys in the summer, while Sis was always done up in blond curls and ribbons. Every day we boys, even Greg who was just two years old, were dressed in freshly pressed shirts and sharp-creased pants, while Sis was always dolled up in crinkly dresses.

Mom herself came from a family of four children, two of whom had been adopted, and practically every kid in the neighborhood had hung out at their house. So, I knew Mom had inherited a soft heart from her parents. On summer evenings, my grandfather had told ghost stories to all the kids on the front porch, and Grandma had fed them pastries made from recipes out of cookbooks she'd brought with her all the way from Germany.

Mom gave in to Henry's passion for model airplanes and engines of all kinds so that the garage was littered with various parts, none of which matched. The house was also full of mechanical junk, at least his room was. As for myself, I got to keep lots of hamsters, guinea pigs, tropical fish, and other pets in the house and several rabbits in hutches in the backyard. Mom also supported Will's seasonal yearning for baseball cards. Scarcely a day went by without his buying more, and through the summer his left cheek was permanently bulged out with a wad of bubblegum. Katie had more than her share of dolls, and, although he was just a toddler, Greg had so many stuffed animals that his room looked like a toy store. Still, I wished Dad were here conducting the interrogation. He had this way of looking at things from a distance, as if he weren't all mixed up in it.

"I hear that her parents are divorced," Mom said, like it was supposed to have some deep meaning.

"Yes," I said dully, for that news had already made the rounds several times.

"And that the girl's father is after them."

"After them?" I asked, suddenly anxious, but not exactly sure what she meant. I had lived in Roscoe long enough to know that, in the absence of exciting news, people tended to make up their own. I guessed that people must have pretty much run out of things to say about Chigger, and had started to concoct some fresh gossip.

"Where did you hear that he's after them?" I asked, a note of challenge in my voice.

"Never mind where I heard it," Mom said, sprinkling water from the pop bottle on one of Dad's shirts. "Just stay away from her."

"Mom!"

"Do what you're told."

Before she could think up anything else to complain about, I went upstairs to my room to look up "delinquent" in the dictionary and be alone with my animals. It wasn't that I particularly wanted to hang out with Chigger. I just thought it was funny that for all their claiming that they didn't want anything to do with the new girl, folks sure bothered themselves a lot about her.

IV.

"THIS IS THE THIRD TIME THIS SPRING I've had to patch these jeans!" Mom told me for the fourth time late one afternoon toward the middle of May. She was stitching the edges of the iron-on patches because you could never count on them holding otherwise, not the way I played kickball, at least that's what Mom always said.

Sitting with her in the living room, I was trying to concentrate on the Mickey Mouse Club, which, because of dark-eyed Annette Funicello, was my favorite show on TV.

Mom bit off the thread. "Now try to be more care—"

"*Frrr-whitt!*"

Abruptly Mom sat up. "What was that?"

I gasped when I saw the small figure on the porch, hands cupped around her eyes like blinders, nose pressed against the screen, as she stared right into our living room.

"*Frrr-whitt!*"

Picking up her feet, Mom glanced around the floor for signs of rodents or insects. "What *is* that? I've never heard anything quite like it before."

Barely able to catch my breath, I mumbled, "It's Chigger."

Mom shook her head. "It's too early for bugs."

"No, at the door."

Mom twisted around in the stuffed chair and jumped. "Oh my God, child! You scared the living daylights out of me!"

"Anybody home?" Chigger asked.

Mom frowned. "You should know as well as anyone, young lady, the way you've been peering through that screen."

"Yes, ma'am."

Mom muttered, "Thank God Luke's father isn't home, traipsing around in his boxer shorts the way he always does."

"Yes, ma'am."

Mom stiffened. Chigger wasn't supposed to have heard that.

Grabbing hold of the white porcelain knob of the screen-door, she started into the house just as naturally as can be, until Mom gave her what Henry, Will, Sis, and I called "the look," which stopped her cold, in mid-step, as well as if a gun was pointed at her nose. "Were you invited into this house, young lady?"

She gulped. "No, ma'am."

For a moment Chigger tottered on one foot as she awaited further instructions.

Mom sighed. "Well, don't just stand there wobbling like a bowling pin that can't make up its mind to fall or not!"

Chigger started back out the door.

"It's too late now! Just come in!"

"Yes, ma'am."

Mom picked up the blue jeans and resumed her work, but not without casting a dark look at the girl. "Next time please mind your manners and knock."

"Yes, ma'am."

"And if not invited in, you should ask, 'May I come in?'"

"Yes, ma'am."

I knew what Mom was thinking about her—in one ear, out the other—but Chigger *was* trying to be polite. I figured she just didn't know how. For a moment she stood there, hands plastered to her sides, then she turned to me and in a stiff, formal manner asked, "You wanna go out and play?"

I stared back at her, wondering all at once what she was doing at my house, how she had found out where I lived, and what Mom was going to say about this unexpected visit.

"Well, you wanna play or not?"

Squirming like a worm, I glanced toward Mom. "Oh, uh, sure, okay, I mean, I guess so."

A deep, almost purple color rose in Mom's face. I knew that later, in the privacy of our home, she was going to give me what for. I wanted to tell her that Chigger just wasn't like normal people. And I wanted to tell Chigger that Mom was this stern only when she had a lot of work to do, but then again she always had clothes to mend, dishes to wash, and a house to clean for seven people. I introduced Chigger as "that new girl in school," although Mom already knew plenty about her.

"Pleased to meet you," said Mom, her eyes still on her mending.

Chigger made a little lopsided curtsy. "Yeah, me too. I mean, yes, ma'am."

Mom put down the jeans and rose stiffly in her practical cotton dress. "Well, I'd better get supper started. Luke, we'll have a talk later this evening, won't we?"

"Yes, ma'am."

I knew that Mom's belief in good manners also applied to herself. She had to be polite to Chigger since she was our guest, even if she had invited herself into our home. Big grin spread across her face, Chigger watched Mom walk out of the room and then she turned to me. "Your mom's real nice, Luke."

"What?" Mom did have her moments, but Chigger hadn't exactly witnessed one of them.

"So, you wanna go out and play or not?"

I glanced longingly at the Mickey Mouse Club, especially at Annette with her dark, bright eyes and mouse-ear cap. Watching TV sure seemed a lot safer than playing with Chigger, plus I had to contend with Mom. But then again, it was a free country, wasn't it, and I had to mind my manners, too.

I sighed. "Okay, what do you want to do?"

"Anything you want, Luke."

Just as I'd feared, she was going to make me, the most boring kid in the fifth grade, decide what to do.

Our sprawling white clapboard house with its high ceilings, winding staircase, and large closets, including the cedar-lined closet in Mom's room, was a wonderful place to play everything from hide-and-seek to cowboys and Indians. Although Dad had nailed shut the laundry chute to protect us from unscheduled trips to the cellar, we still had lots of places in which to play all kinds of games.

Chigger gazed in awe at the house with its many rooms, oak woodwork, bright flowered wallpaper, and especially the cut-glass chandelier over the dining room table.

"It makes little rainbows," she said, head tilted backward, her mouth hung so wide open that I thought her jaw might become unhinged.

"Yeah," I said, not knowing what else to say to her. "They're prisms."

"Say what?" Chigger asked.

Usually when I had a friend over, Mom would chase us from the house, calling, "I don't want you kids underfoot. Go outside and play. You can use the fresh air and exercise." But today she called from the kitchen, "Don't stray far, Luke. In fact, you better stick around the yard, you hear me?"

At the sound of Mom's voice Chigger sprang toward the door, turning back to me just long enough to urge, "Come on, dreamboat!"

Through the kitchen doorway I saw Mom freeze, and I hurried out of the house, not so much to be with Chigger, but to avoid some boring chore which I knew she was now trying to think up to keep me from playing with my new classmate.

Chigger was already rocking back and forth on the porch swing. Glancing back over her shoulder, she asked, "What kept you, slowpoke?"

"What's this, uh, dreamboat stuff?" I asked, red-faced, worrying that if I wasn't careful, she might pop me like she had Buzz. But she just made these gooey eyes at me, like in the previews of the kinds of movies we made fun of at the Palace and which we weren't old enough to see anyway. "Well, quit it," I said. "It's stupid. And don't go saying that…that stuff to me like you have been at school."

"Anything you say, Luke."

She sure was showing a more peaceful and agreeable side from the one on display at school. She almost seemed like a girl, which worried me no end. I wanted to ask her to leave, but I figured I'd only feel worse if I hurt her feelings. I was in what Dad called "a dilemma," at least I thought I was, because with Chigger you could never be quite sure where you were. I began to envy Buzz for just getting his nose punched.

I sat down with her on the porch swing and we swayed back and forth, both of us slumped down, our toes scuffing the floor. I was afraid she was going to ask again, "What do you want to do?" and I'd say, "Just swing back and forth," and she'd call me an old grandpa.

Buzz and the other guys had already made fun of me for leading a dull life because I was often content just to sit on the front porch and feel myself being alive. They were more interested in souping up their bicycles with decals and streamers or revving them up with playing cards pinned across the spokes with clothespins. They liked to watch *King Kong* and other scary movies at the Palace, which terrified me, and when they bought candy down at the grocery they called me a weirdo because, like my dad, I didn't have much of a sweet tooth. They accused me of being a "nature nut" because I liked to look for insects under tree stumps, peer into doves' nests at the ivory-white eggs, or poke around the fields at the edge of town looking for cottontail rabbits.

Laying her head back against the swing, Chigger asked, "What do you do for fun around here?"

I licked my lips nervously. "Well, uh, you wanna see my fish?"

I expected her to burst out laughing, but she only screwed up her face. "Fish?"

My face was becoming permanently red. "Yeah, I've got tropical fish." Actually, I had five aquariums of various sizes stocked with every kind of tropical fish available between Roscoe and Louisville. I didn't know if it was proper to show a girl your fish, but with nothing else to do we slipped back into the house, tiptoeing up the creaky stairs so Mom wouldn't be unduly roused.

My aquariums were filled with guppies, mollies, platys, swordtails, neon tetras, zebra danios, and other freshwater tropical fish. I had a large bowl of goldfish, too. By way of warm-blooded animals I had guinea pigs and hamsters in my room, as well as the rabbits in hutches in the backyard. I also had box turtles, lizards, and a corn snake to keep Sis out of my room.

Since neither Henry nor Will cared to associate with the animals, at least in those quantities, I got to have my own room. Mom wasn't too fond of the animals herself, so I had to clean the room myself. I didn't mind this at all, because when you had a mom like mine you learned to appreciate your privacy. She did keep Bump, our green parakeet, downstairs in the kitchen "for company," but as far as I could see all he ever did was eat and squawk.

Chigger strolled into the room, agog. "Man, you got your own pet store!"

"Sort of." I tried to look humble, but inside I was fit to burst with pride.

Chigger sat in front of the largest forty-gallon aquarium, just staring through the glass.

Finally I felt obliged to ask, "What are you doing?"

"It's like being in a dream."

"What do you mean?"

"A dream—one I'd like to be in, with everything just floating around as easy as can be. Not a worry in the world."

I couldn't disagree with her since I liked to sit before the aquariums so much that Mom often said in disbelief, "I think you'd rather watch those fish than TV."

"Wouldn't you like to step right inside your dreams?" Chigger asked. "And never, ever have to come back to the real world?"

"Yeah, sure," I said, although I'd surely want to come back to my family. I would've gone for the adventure of it, but it seemed she really wanted to vanish forever into another place.

We visited with the animals for a while, Chigger turning in circles, exclaiming every two seconds, "Man, you got it made! What I wouldn't give to have all these animals! Well, maybe all of them except for that snake over there. Them slithery things give me the heebie-jeebies."

I didn't point out that it was a lot of work cleaning up after so many animals.

"My mom won't even let me have a kitten," she sighed.

"We've got two—Blackie and Midnight. They're both black."

"Wow!"

The funny thing about Chigger was that as drawn

as she was to the animals she seemed almost scared to pet them, like she was afraid a guinea pig might maul her.

"Maybe your mom would let you have a goldfish," I suggested. "They're real quiet and easy to get along with."

Chigger shook her head. "She says all they do is up and croak."

"Not if you condition the water."

She looked blankly at me. "Condition?"

"Yeah, treat it with stuff to get out the chlorine."

"Chlorine?"

"Yes, it's—"

"Oh, yeah, I know all about that stuff."

We stood looking at each other a minute, then I said, "Uh, well, I do have an extra goldfish, if you ever want him."

"Wouldn't he be lonely?"

"Okay, you can have two."

She eyed me, as if thinking, what's the hitch, and said, "I'll have to ask my mom."

Then we went out in the yard where I told her about Blackie and Midnight since I couldn't find them. "They were the last two kittens in the litter. Everybody wanted the pretty calico ones, the white ones, and the tiger-striped one, but the black ones weren't just bad luck, they were common." I didn't tell her outright that the reason I wanted them was because nobody else did.

"You sure are nuts about animals," she said.

I blushed, but not too much now, because I could see that Chigger herself liked the animals.

I showed her Ginger, Biscuit, Sugar, Bunsley, Opal, and the other rabbits in the hutches by the fence in the backyard, which Mrs. Filbert, the old lady who lived next door to us, was always complaining about, although they hardly smelled, at least not too much, and as everybody knows, rabbits are pretty quiet.

"You ought to be on *Zoo Parade*," suggested Chigger.

Thinking of awkward Marlin Perkins, I wasn't too crazy about the idea. "Actually, I'm going to be a veterinarian."

Chigger got this puzzled look.

"An animal doctor," I explained.

"Oh, yeah. Sure. I knew that."

Carefully opening the door to one hutch, I showed her Sugar's baby rabbits, pink as bubblegum, in a nest of fur.

Chigger reached in to pet them with her forefinger.

"Better not touch them," I said. "Their mother won't like the smell of people on them."

Chigger snorted. "I sure know what she means."

Although I had a pretty good idea what she was talking about, I asked, "What?"

She smirked. "I like animals a whole lot better than people. That's all."

"Me, too," I said as she suddenly turned and ran back around the house. I found her on the front porch, again gliding back and forth on the swing. She looked off into the maple trees. "It's real peaceful here, ain't it, Luke?"

"Sure is."

It was one of my favorite places in the world, up there on the swing on the screened-in porch without a care in the world, just gliding back and forth, looking out over Milford Boulevard, the two-lane brick street lined with maple trees. "Just counting the cars," Dad often joked. Most nights we were lucky if three vehicles rolled by.

I started to join Chigger on the porch, but she ran off again to the rope swing dangling from the sycamore tree in the backyard, and I had a terrible thought. Maybe she was getting all hopped up and fidgety, like at school. I found her sitting on the notched board swing.

"What kept you?" she asked as I arrived, out of breath.

Before I could answer she climbed the tree. Tottering out onto the branch on which the rope swing was tied, about ten feet above the ground, she called out, "Look, no hands!"

I didn't know whether to think she was being dangerous or stupid, especially when I followed her. With her wiry arms and legs, she climbed all over the tree; then hung upside down on the branch.

"Watch me skin the cat!"

"It's too high!"

Grabbing the branch with both hands she twisted; then dropped to the ground, landing feet first, but with quite a jar.

"You okay?" I asked.

Her smile got very big. "Sure, it ain't nothin' but a dumb ol' tree." And she climbed back up again, urging me, "Come on, you do it!"

"No."

"Scaredy-cat!"

I looked down at the ground, which appeared to be spinning around in wavy circles. I couldn't disagree with her because I was afraid of pretty much everything—heights, the dark, annual immunization shots at Doc Phillips' office, monster movies, and rides at the county fair.

"Come on, fraidy-cat!"

I shook my head. "I'm just not good at these things." I was big and strong for my age, but had such an active imagination that I saw tragedy in most every situation. Just looking down at the ground I saw myself in a body cast. Walking home from the park at night I imagined icy hands clamped around my neck, and constantly I had visions of my father and his plane falling out of the sky.

Chigger dropped her challenge and, feeling dizzy up in that tree, I tried to change the subject. "Where do you live?" I asked.

"Over there." She waved back toward the boulevard, sunk deeply in the late afternoon shade, her gesture taking in most of the neighborhood.

"But where?" I had seen no "For sale" signs in front of any houses, not for months.

"Just over there," she said irritably. "By the key shop."

"Well, how did you know where I lived?"

She snorted. "I looked in the phone book. Ain't too many Zielinskis in this here town."

"Luke!" Mom called. "Time to wash up for supper!"

Knowing Dad would be home soon, I eagerly climbed down from the tree, just in time to see Chigger jump from the lowest branch. I cried, "Be careful!"

"Oh, don't be such a worrywart!"

She was just the opposite of me. It was as if she didn't particularly care what happened to her, even if she got hurt.

I turned toward the house. "I gotta go."

She shrugged. "Sure."

If she were one of my regular friends, I would have asked Mom if she could stay for dinner. Mom absolutely loved to feed people, but somehow I knew it was different with Chigger. Looking back at her, just about tripping over a tree root, I called, "'Bye."

"See you at school."

I stopped cold. How was I supposed to act around her in front of the guys? Chigger peered deeply at me, like she had the eyes of a cat in the evening. A light flicked on in our kitchen.

"I gotta go," I emphasized.

"You're nice," she called across the yard, just as I reached the back porch.

The words sticking in my throat, I called back to her, "So are you."

When I went into the house she was still out there, hanging around in the dusk, like she had no where else to go.

V.

MONDAY MORNING OF THE LAST WEEK of school, Buzz poked me across the aisle to remark once again, "Ain't she a dope and a half?"

Judging from her schoolwork and Mrs. Simpson's clucking and shaking her head as they went over her assignments, Chigger wasn't even close to being smart, at least in school. I thought of telling Buzz that, as a C-minus student himself, he shouldn't talk. "She's not so bad," I said. "Mrs. Simpson says she just needs a lot of individual attention until she catches up."

Gilman shook his head. "She ought to be held back. She'll never catch up with us."

Buzz nodded. "You know, she's been here a whole month practically and she still doesn't have a friend in the world."

I flinched, because every afternoon of the past week Chigger and I had played together in my backyard, in secret. When we were at school she never let on that she knew me. But after school she came by and we climbed the sycamore tree and ran down rabbit trails in the field just behind our house near the edge of town, not far from the Co-op hatchery. We steered clear of downtown on purpose, not only because boys weren't supposed to play with girls, but also because nobody in Roscoe was supposed to hang out with Chigger. Fortunately, we preferred the wilds of the pasture, except for the occasional cow-pie and some worries about an ill-humored Hereford bull named Lucifer.

I felt ashamed about keeping our friendship a secret. The guys were already asking me about what I was doing every afternoon, and I was glad that the school year was almost over. We were on the verge of a whole summer of swimming at the municipal pool, bicycling around town, going for ice cream at the Tastee Freez, watching movies at the Palace Theater, saving up for cherry Cokes at the Roscoe Cigar Store and Fountain, and playing baseball at the Boys' Club.

Of course, Mom had had a fit about my hanging around with Chigger. But she also had that big, squishy heart of hers. So, just as I got to keep my vast number of pets, I got to have Chigger as a friend, at least temporarily; that is, until I could find a polite way of ditching her.

All that last week of school the girls squealed at all our idiotic jokes, most of which came from Buzz. None of the guys got into any fights, and even Buzz was in a good mood, at least most of the time.

For me, the week passed like a dream, especially the magical last day. We cleaned out our desks, happily depositing wrinkled papers, stubs of pencils, empty fountain pen cartridges, and other debris from our year in the fifth grade into a large wastebasket we slid up and down the aisles. Finally the bell rang and we went screaming into the free world, waving report cards and papers from last November, which Mrs. Simpson had found when she had cleaned out her own desk.

"School's out! School's out! Teacher let the monkeys out!"

I got hold of my senses just long enough to glance around for Chigger, but, true to her independent nature, she had already made herself scarce and departed for regions unknown. That was all right with me, because like the poet I was accused of being, I needed to feel things from deep within me to the very tips of my fingers and toes, and to do that I sometimes had to be alone.

I remained in my dream for the rest of that day and well into the next morning. On that first official full day of vacation I stepped outside carefully, afraid that it might really *be* a dream, that if I made any sudden moves it would vanish like a rabbit into the brush and I would wake up to a whole face-full of schoolbooks. I looked down at my feet. They were still there in clean white tennis shoes, which Mom had bought in perfect timing with the warm days of early summer.

The change of seasons could be divided into two parts—the first in early spring when we exchanged clunky parkas for windbreakers, after which we wondered how we'd ever gotten through the winter in those stiff, awkward coats that seemed like they were weighted with lead. The second part was when we traded our crusty old leather shoes for supple new sneakers.

I ran zigzag around the yard for a while, enjoying the feel of the wind that swirled around me. With the lighter shoes I was pretty certain I could fly, and even tried a few times. They remained white for only a few seconds; yet I knew that the smell of new canvas would carry me clear through to September.

I spent all morning just poking around the yard, enjoying the good weather. When I came in for lunch at noon Mom said, "You don't know how lucky you are that you don't have to work." But I did know. We all knew—my brothers, my sister, my classmates, all of Rutherford B. Hayes Grade School and every other kid in North America.

Mom asked, "I suppose your little friend left for the summer?"

"I don't think so."

"That's too bad."

Gulping down the rest of my root beer Kool-Aid, I put the glass on the kitchen counter, caught a breath, and said, "She'll probably be over any time now."

Stuck with her own good manners, Mom grumbled, "She comes over more than enough to make a pest of herself."

I wiped my forearm across my mouth. "She's hardly any trouble at all, and she's been real polite."

"She always overstays her welcome, right into our dinner hour."

"Well, maybe we ought to ask her to eat with us sometime."

Mom pretended not to hear me. "Doesn't she have a home of her own?"

"Sure she does!" I answered brightly, although I still didn't know where it was, not exactly. She just said she lived in an apartment in a white house near the key shop, and since I wasn't quite sure what an apartment was until I looked it up in the dictionary, I hadn't asked her any more questions.

Before Mom could bug me any more I ran outside again to inspect the trees for bird nests. Then I made a tour of the yard to see what flowers were coming into bloom everywhere—daffodils, tulips, and irises. I paused to smell the blue-lipped irises, going from flower to flower sticking my nose in each one.

"Hey, Professor!"

In sudden terror, I straightened just as Buzz, Toby, and Gilman rode into the backyard on their bikes.

"What are you doing?" asked Buzz.

I mumbled, "Uh, I'm gardening."

Buzz made a face. "With your nose?"

I wiped my hands on my jeans and tried to think of a more convincing answer. "I was checking for bugs."

"Sure you were. You were smelling flowers—just like a girl!"

"Well, I…."

Toby asked, "Where you been hiding yourself?"

Glad that they had dropped the subject of flowers, I mumbled, "Nowhere in particular."

"Been taking care of all those animals? You ought to be a zookeeper," Buzz told me.

That idea had crossed my mind, more than once.

"Hey, we're goin' alley-hunting. You wanna go?" Gilman asked.

"Hot diggity dog!" I exclaimed. What a way to start the summer! Alley-hunting did place us in direct competition with Fred the Junkman, as Dad said, but we found the most amazing treasures. Last summer I'd dug a one-armed Panda out of a trashcan (why anyone would want to throw it away I couldn't imagine) and Buzz had found a roller skate. It didn't matter that, not knowing where it had come from, Mom wouldn't allow the grimy bear into the house, even as a gift for Greg, or that Buzz was still looking for the other skate. We had found *treasure*.

My eyes lit up at the prospect of being an entrepreneur, as Dad had called us last summer, although

I wasn't sure what he meant by the term even after I'd looked it up. "Let me get my bike!"

"Ya-hooo!" Toby whooped. Buzz and Gilman waved their arms like cowboys on wild broncos as they rode their bikes in wobbly circles in the yard. Then suddenly they jammed on their brakes and froze, just like they were in an episode of *The Twilight Zone*. I don't know who saw whom first—Chigger, who was tearing across the yard toward our porch, or the guys.

Buzz made a face. "What's *she* doing here?"

"She lives over there somewhere." I said, waving my arm in the general direction of Brown County.

"And you let her cut through your yard?"

"Why not?"

Gilman snorted. "Probably kill all the grass."

Without a word to any of us Chigger trotted over to the sycamore tree, climbed onto the first branch, and proceeded to show off, balancing herself on one leg, jumping up and down, and finally skinning the cat. They laughed when she landed too hard.

Angrily she whirled around. "See if you can do any better!"

"I ain't doing nothin' with you," Buzz told her.

Toby urged, "Tell her to get away from your tree, Luke."

"Yeah," Gilman said. "Tell her to get lost. This is *your* yard. She's trespassing."

"I, uh, well, you know, she's not hurting anything," I stammered.

They gawked at me. "Come on, what's the matter with you? Tell her to beat it!"

I said lamely, "She's real good at climbing."

"That's probably because she's part monkey," Toby said.

"Yeah, she even smells like a monkey," added Gilman.

"She does not."

Buzz squinted at me. "What's with you?"

"Nothing," I said, shuffling. Actually Chigger did smell a little funny sometimes, but I told the guys, "It's not right to say mean things about a person."

"But she's not a person," Buzz claimed. "She's a monkey."

Scratching themselves under the arms, they mimicked apes for a while, at which they were surprisingly good, especially Gilman. Then suddenly Buzz jabbed a finger at me. "You like her!"

"Do not."

"Do too!"

"Do not!"

"Then what's she doing at your house?"

"Just visiting."

They were shocked by my 'fessing up. His neck lengthening, his mouth hung open, Buzz peered deeply at me. "You mean you *let* her come over to your house and everything? You mean you really been hanging out with her?"

I shrugged. "Sometimes."

"That ain't right," said Toby, shaking his head in disbelief. "Not with her."

"She's not so bad."

They began to chant, "Luke's got a girlfriend!"

My fists closed and my face got hot. "Knock it off."

"Well, you do, don't you?" challenged Buzz.

"She's not my girlfriend, but yeah, I do like her," I said. "She may act stupid at school, but she's nice, sort of, when you get to know her."

Buzz stepped back, his nose wrinkling up like he was in the process of smelling something really awful. "Did you say you *like* her?"

I swallowed. "Yeah, I like her. You wanna make something of it?"

My whole summer flashed before my eyes—being part of the gang, having a proper home, being accepted in Roscoe, being a traitor to Chigger. Honor and treason, my father had said, the world is full of both. So is the fifth grade. He also had said that all's fair in love and war, when it should be just the opposite, which I'd never understood until now. Like any normal kid I didn't get along all that well with my own brothers, especially Henry, and truth be told the guys weren't much to brag about, but they were my only buddies and I didn't want to lose them.

Buzz's chin thrust forward. "How do you want it—fistfight, wrestle, combination, or anything goes?"

I shrugged. "Whatever you want."

He must have picked "anything goes" because suddenly he jumped on me: snorting, grappling, punching, and kicking all at once. "No biting!" was the only rule mentioned, but I don't know who said it—Toby, Gilman, or it might even have been Buzz. I wasn't familiar with any formal rules for fighting, and having a brother two years older and considerably larger than myself, I wasn't too interested in combat. But I was the biggest kid in my class and, once stuck in a fight, I wasn't about to lose to anybody, especially to the likes of Buzz Phillips.

With one flip—which happened so fast Buzz must have been embarrassed—I had him on the ground. Sitting on his stomach, I pinned his hands on either side of his head Indian-style.

"Spit on him!" Toby urged me.

"What?" I asked in disbelief.

"Spit on him!"

"Yeah, go ahead," agreed Gilman, licking his lips eagerly. "Spit on him!"

Henry occasionally employed this technique for humiliating me when I was similarly pinned, forming the bubbly spit in his mouth and slowly letting the glob slide from his lips right into my face.

Struggling furiously, Buzz hollered at Toby and Gilman, "Shut up, you guys! You don't have to give him any ideas!"

Toby shrugged. "That's just one of the rules."

"No, it's not!" Buzz screamed. "It's optional. He doesn't have to! It's only if he wants to."

"But we got to tell him what his rights are," said Gilman.

"No, you don't!"

Toby and Gilman put on innocent faces, but I sensed that they were looking forward to a real bloodbath…or spit bath. I also sensed that they were making up the rules as they went along. Believing in a more civilized code of combat, I asked Buzz, "Say uncle?" He answered by pushing against me so hard I thought his head would explode like a water balloon. "Come on, be a pal, say uncle. Please?" Buzz continued to struggle without a chance of dislodging me. If nothing else, I was heavy. Finally I looked to Toby and Gilman for help.

"Tell you what, we'll count to twelve o'clock," Toby said to me, "and when we reach midnight Buzz is the loser."

"That ain't one of the rules!" howled Buzz, but I was glad when Gilman began to count. Buzz thrashed furiously, but wasn't able to budge me. At eleven o'clock I let him go.

"What are you doing?" Toby shrieked. "You coulda beat him!"

As far as I was concerned I had already whooped Buzz, but I hoped to save our friendship. However, as he brushed himself off, he snarled at me, "You're a dope, Zielinski!"

They got on their bikes, calling, "So long, sucker. Have a great summer—with her!"

I watched them pedal into the distance, squabbling among themselves.

"You didn't have to tell him to spit," Buzz complained.

"Well, he could have if he wanted to," Toby answered. "I was just telling him what was fair. Next time get somebody else to referee."

"I sure as heck will!"

"What about me?" Gilman asked. "I'll referee."

"You aren't any better'n him!"

I was already missing them.

I stood there looking after them while Chigger continued to drift back and forth on the swing. I wanted to go back into the house, to forget both her and the guys, to just hang out with my animals and read books. Instead, not sure what I was doing, I went over to the sycamore tree.

"You're nice, too," she said immediately.

"What?"

"You said I was nice, right in front of those jerks."

As I recalled, I had said she was sort of nice, but she acted like it was the greatest thing anybody had ever said about her. I wondered why she hadn't stuck up for herself, but then I saw it in her eyes, that "you're my hero" look. I got a sick feeling in the bottom of my stomach.

Then Chigger reared up. "But I ain't stupid!"

"I never said you...I just said you act stu...I mean...oh forget it!"

She must have agreed that it was a touchy subject because she dropped it, and we hung around the tree for a while, not saying much to each other. I kept thinking, this isn't how I want to spend my summer. Then Dad came home early in his tan uniform, bright with insignia, which was a real treat for us. Usually, he worked such long hours we hardly ever saw him. Whooping and hollering, Henry, Will, Sis, and I ran to greet him. He scooped Sis up in his arms and asked us, "Now what kind of mischief have you kids been up to today?"

No one volunteered any information.

"I get it," Dad said. "Name, rank, and serial number only."

"We're home for summer vacation," Sis declared not only to Dad, but also to half the neighborhood.

"Vacation," he muttered the word as though recalling some vague memory. He'd brought us presents as he had on other special occasions: a model airplane kit for Henry, a bag of marbles for Will, a Mrs. Potato Head for Sis, a stuffed mouse for Greg, who was in the house with Mom, and a live fire-belly newt for me. "Thought I'd get you all something to start off the summer right."

As usual I held back, by nature an observer. He tousled my hair. "What's for dinner, Professor?"

"Fried chicken, I think."

He often said I had the brains *and* the appetite

in the family. Glancing across the yard to the sycamore tree, he asked, "Who's your girlfriend, Luke?"

I frowned. "She's not my girlfriend."

"Sure, she isn't!" teased Henry.

"My sweetheart," Will mocked, opening his arms in a wide embrace.

"Cut it out!"

"Why don't you invite your friend over," Dad suggested.

Reluctantly, I waved to Chigger.

She got up from the swing, took a step toward us; then she ran in the opposite direction, back toward her own home, wherever that was.

That afternoon I hung around in my room observing my newt until dinner, after which the whole family sat on the front porch, Mom and Dad rocking back and forth on the swing.

"What're you doing, Henry?" asked Sis.

Considering my brothers, sister, and myself so beneath him that he needn't recognize our existence, Henry continued to read his book.

Sis turned to Mom. "What's Henry doing, huh, Mom?"

"The summer reading program started at the public library today," Mom explained. "This year whoever reads the most books gets a model of an Indianapolis 500 racecar."

Henry continued to rapidly scan the pages of his book. He could give a wart about books, but with his mechanical bent, he was crazy for that car. That morning he'd checked out twenty books from the library—the maximum allowed—and had blazed through most of them already. He didn't exactly bother to read them. He just looked for the story line and memorized the names of the main characters long enough to report them to Mrs. Lovington, the children's librarian.

I was just the opposite. I loved books and read one book after another throughout the long winter. But during warm weather, at least during the daylight hours, I preferred to be outside where I could rely directly on my five senses.

"Looks like Henry is in the Indy 500 himself," Dad said.

Although it hadn't been openly mentioned, since it was officially summer vacation we were all on the front porch for one reason, as we had been during the past three summers in Roscoe. As the evening went by, however, I began to worry that it might not happen yet this season. Maybe it wasn't warm enough. Maybe that second helping had made Mom and Dad lose interest in dessert, although that would be hard to imagine, at least for Mom.

Toward dusk Dad leaned back and yawned. "What d'you say we go in and see what's on TV."

"Aw!" Henry, Will, Sis, Greg, and I groaned in harmony.

Dad looked off into the sunset. "'Course, I do feel like a little dessert. How 'bout you guys?"

There was instant chaos on the front porch. Mrs. Filbert must have thought that our offbeat military family had gone to war among ourselves. At that moment I knew that the summer had truly come again.

Dad gave me a dollar and a quarter and the use of Sis's bicycle. From there we knew the routine. My blond, curly-headed brother, Will, climbed onto the handlebars and we cruised down the boulevard, making a leisurely trip along the tree-lined street, then a left onto Poplar Street for two blocks and we were at the Tastee Freez.

With an air of importance I ordered seven ice cream cones. We often joked about getting an extra one for the eighth hole in the two paper trays to better balance them, but Dad, the diplomat, always said there'd be too much fighting over it.

The counter girl placed the seven cones in the trays, and racing against the heat, dodging potholes and nearsighted motorists, I pedaled furiously back home. Poised heroically on the handlebars, Will fulfilled his one assignment of carrying the ice cream. With both hands occupied with the trays and my pedaling like a maniac, he faced quite a challenge just staying on the bike, let alone disembarking when we arrived back at the house.

Over the past three summers we had tried various methods and had perfected the following technique. As I slowed down in the side yard, Will made a running leap off the bicycle with the understanding that he was to balance and protect the ice cream cones, even at the risk of his own life. Then, jumping off myself, I sort of let the bike roll along and park itself on its side in the bushes, its rear tire spinning crazily.

"What was that noise?" Mom asked as we rounded the corner of the house.

I shrugged. "Bike sort of got away from me."

"My bike!" shrieked Sis, making a monster face at me.

For risking his neck Will had the honor of serving the ice cream cones, but I was allowed to keep the change, which was always twenty cents.

"Ought to get an extra ice cream cone tomorrow,"

suggested Will as usual. "It'd be easier for me to carry the trays."

Dad asked, "Who'd eat it?"

"Me!" Will said. "As a reward for carrying them."

"Hazardous duty?" Raising his eyebrows, Dad pondered that argument.

Glancing up from his book, Henry reminded him, "But I'm the oldest!"

"I'm the smartest!" I claimed, knowing that would really bug Henry.

"Well, I'm the only girl in the family," Sis claimed. "And I don't go around fighting all the time like you guys."

As usual Dad "took the matter under advisement" and we dug into our desserts. There was nothing like savoring that ice cream in the dusk growing around us, and I told myself that I could forget my fight with Buzz. I could forget Chigger. I could forget everything, as Mom and Dad swung back and forth, back and forth into the ease and comfort of summer.

VI.

THE NEXT MORNING CHIGGER SHOWED UP at my house
again. Pretty much ignoring me, she climbed the
sycamore tree, raced Sis's bike down Milford Boulevard
(without so much as asking permission to use it), and
did cartwheels in the front yard. Still moping about the
loss of my other friends, I hung around because I had
nothing better to do. I didn't really mind her being there
until she began to tease me. "I can climb higher than
you, Luke. Come on, see if you can do any better."

"No, thanks."

"Well then, let's see who can do the most
cartwheels."

"I can't do cartwheels."

She stopped cold. "What do you mean you can't
do cartwheels? Anybody can do cartwheels."

I shook my head. "I get dizzy being upside
down."

"Then I'll race you to the corner. Come on!"

I might be scared of my own shadow, but the
two things I could do were fight and run, which Dad
said complemented each other really well. "You'll never
know when you might need one or the other."

Chigger leaned forward. "On your mark, get set,
GO!"

She fudged on the start, but I easily caught up and raced past her. When she got to the finish a few seconds later she quickly touched the tree and blurted, "I meant to the tree and back."

"Hey! No fair!" I shouted.

Getting the jump on me again, she darted back toward our starting place, but I zipped right past her. As soon as we'd stopped, out of breath, she exclaimed, "Race you again!"

I shook my head.

"Come on!"

"There's no point in it."

"Well then, you lose."

"No, I don't. I won fair and square."

She squirmed. "Well, I can climb higher than you. I can—"

"There are lots of things you can do better than me," I said. "But there are some things I can do better. That's just life. You don't always have to outdo everybody else."

"Yes, I do."

I frowned. "Let's stop, you know, competing. Just consider us even now."

Still getting her breath back, she looked at me like she didn't have a clue what I meant. Then she asked, "Where'd you learn to run like that?"

I shrugged. "Dad says I'm a natural."

"Well, if you can run so good and you can stomp Buzz Phillips like he was a little piss-ant, how come you're so scared of everything?"

"I'm not scared of anything."

"Oh, yeah? Like I ain't a girl."

Briefly, I pondered her claim.

Then she told me point-blank, "I'd say you're one

pretty weird guy, Luke. You're always off somewheres else."

"What do you mean?" I asked. "I've been here all morning."

"I mean in your head—you're just like a dumb ol' poet."

I stopped cold. "Where did you hear that? About me being a poet?"

She shrugged. "It ain't like it's a big secret or nothin'."

"It's almost noon," I grumbled. "Don't you have to go home for lunch?"

A hurt look came into her eyes and she said, "Oh, sure. I'm just about starved."

When she left I went into the house and had one of Mom's good home-cooked meals, which for some reason she served extra piping hot in the summer. I tried to tell myself that if Chigger would just leave me alone I would be content to hang around the house all summer and read books and conduct Mr. Wizard experiments. However, an hour later, she was at my door again, asking, "You wanna go to a movie?"

I couldn't think of the name of the movie currently showing at the Palace Theater, but knew it was designed to scare the living daylights out of people.

I looked down at my feet. "Uh, I don't know. My mom said I should stick around the house."

"Why?"

"In case there's an emergency."

"Ain't nothin' gonna happen."

"You never know."

"Those kind of things only happen in the newspaper. You're just chicken."

"Am not!"

"Plock, plock, plock...."

"I might, uh, catch a nasty cold in all that air conditioning."

Throwing her weight onto her left hip, Chigger squinted at me. "Are you out of your mind or what?"

I swallowed. "Well, don't you know in the summer you're supposed to spend as much time outside as you can? It's a lot healthier."

"Are you comin' or not?"

"I'll...I'll have to ask my mom."

I was sure Mom wouldn't want me to go anywhere with Chigger. But I'd forgotten that, with five of us underfoot in the summer, she was all for going to the movies or just about anything else that would get us out of the house. She still didn't like my hanging around with Chigger, but she did have that big, squishy heart, and, thanks to Dad, we'd always followed the rule, "Live and let live," meaning we shouldn't be unkind to Chigger even if she was weird. I was in and out of the house in less than two seconds.

"Well?" Chigger asked.

"She said not to come back until dinnertime."

"Yahoo! Let's go!"

As we strolled along Milford Boulevard I kept thinking that, except for the impending horror movie, it was a pretty day. Leafy branches scattered shadows on the sidewalk, a cardinal called from the very top of a tree, and flowers were popping out everywhere.

"What are you doing?" Chigger asked.

"Nothing," I said. "Just feeling the wind on my face."

Chigger screwed up her nose. "You're hopeless."

"Listen," I said, letting my anger rise up in me. "I don't know what's gotten into you, but you don't have to hang out with me if you don't want to."

"You'd like that, wouldn't you? Then you could hang out with Buzz and Toby and Gilman who are so peachy keen."

"That isn't it, at least not exactly."

"What is it then?"

I didn't dare tell her that I was terrified of horror movies. As we walked along under the canopy of trees I twirled winged maple seeds, picked dandelions, and peered into ant holes.

"Quit your stallin'!"

"I'm not," I said honestly. "It just takes me a long time to get anywhere." After a good rain I went up and down the sidewalk returning stranded worms to the moist grass. I knew every bird's nest in the neighborhood, and as Buzz and the guys and just about everybody in the world knew, I couldn't resist smelling flowers, even dandelions.

"Why would I want to stall?" I asked Chigger.

"Prob'ly 'cuz you're scared of the dark, too."

Since I was in fact afraid of the dark, I didn't say anything.

For a moment Chigger became engrossed in the sidewalk. "Step on a crack, break your mother's back."

I tried to steer the conversation back to a more pleasant subject. "Nice day, isn't it? Real sunny."

"Sure is."

"Seems a shame to waste it."

She squinted at me, hard.

"I mean, to be cooped up all afternoon in a dark theater."

"It's the matinee. Only costs a quarter. Besides, will your mom let you go out to a movie at night?"

"No, I have to be home by dark."

"Well, we ain't got no other choice then, do we?"

Before I could think of any more excuses we were downtown, on Main Street. There was a long line in front of the Palace, indicating an especially scary movie. The poster in the glass window showed chalk-white corpses marching stiffly down a city street in pursuit of wide-eyed, shrieking people.

"This is gonna be great!" Chigger exclaimed.

I reached down, thinking that, if I held onto my stomach real tight, it might quit jumping around on me.

"What's the matter? You hungry?"

"No!" Food was absolutely the last thing on my mind. "It, uh, looks like a pretty good show."

"What'd I tell you?" She slugged me on the arm. "I knew you'd come around to your senses once we got here. No normal red-bloodied American can resist a scary movie."

As the line inched forward I thought my knees were going to buckle under me. Chigger got jumpier, like a jack-in-a-box. "What's holding them up? I can't hardly stand it no more!" She cupped her hands around her mouth and hollered, "Get a move on it up there! We don' wanna miss the previews!"

Everybody turned around and stared at us.

I mentioned gently, "Maybe they sold out."

Instantly she turned on me. I was sure she was going to tear my head off. "They couldn't've! That would be the dirtiest, meanest, lowest down trick of all time!"

Finally we arrived at the window, got our tickets from a bored, gum-chewing high school girl, and entered through the glass doors.

Chigger wiped her brow. "Whew, you had me

scared there for a second."

I tried to smile, but my teeth wouldn't stop clicking together.

Then I heard the ticket girl announce to the kids right behind us, "Sold out!"

Chigger's eyes lit up. "Tough luck, suckers!"

Kids behind us groaned, but not as much as me.

Chigger punched me on the arm again. "We're sure lucky today, ain't we, Luke?"

I faked a smile. "You bet."

As I handed my ticket to the usher I squirmed.

"What's the matter?"

"I gotta go pee."

Chigger gave me the stink-eye.

I squeaked, "No, I really have to go. Bad." Hobbling fast as I could across the lobby to the restroom, I got inside just in time to unzip and aim the stream into the urinal. Suddenly I realized that I could spend the whole movie in there and Chigger couldn't do a thing about it.

Then there came a loud banging on the door. "Hey, Luke! Get a move on it! We're gonna miss the cartoon!"

The other guys in there smirked at me. A high school kid asked, "That your girlfriend?"

"No way!"

"Come on, Luke. Get your butt out here! Now!"

"Ain't no place sacred?" asked the high school kid.

I walked out into the lobby feeling every eye upon me.

"It's about time, slowpoke," she said, yanking me by the arm.

I bent toward her ear as we crossed the lobby

and told her, "You don't have to talk so loud."

"Well, you don't ever act like you're hearing me!"

I wondered if she ever wondered why.

At the glass concessions counter Chigger ordered a tub of buttered popcorn, a large root beer, a Sugar Daddy, and boxes of Jujubes and Good n' Plenty. I started to offer to help pay for the stuff when she turned to me and asked, "You gettin' anything?"

I settled for a box of Milk Duds, plus a Coke to help dissolve the sticky candy out of my teeth.

As we passed through the velvety maroon curtains that separated the lobby area from the dark part of the theater, Chigger exclaimed, "Dang!"

I jumped, imagining a pair of ice-cold hands tightening around my neck. "What's the matter now?"

She pointed to the sign: BALCONY CLOSED. "Must be filled up already."

I shook my head. "They won't let kids up there anymore, not since *The Blob*."

Chigger's eyes got bright as crystal. "I seen that movie. It's about that big purple glob of Jell-o that absorbs people, bones and all! What happened? Did somebody fall out of the balcony and get kilt?"

"Some guys...." I didn't mention Buzz, Toby, and Gilman, knowing what Chigger thought of them. "Some guys brought a jar of grape jelly to the movie and started flicking it down on people from the balcony. After a while people started screaming and then they ran out of the theater right in the middle of the movie."

Chigger's face got this religious look. "*Nothin'* would scare me out of that movie. It was—what do they call it—a masterpiece."

I just looked at her, as usual amazed and

perplexed.

"Hey, you wanna sit down in front?"

I was in such a trance that I hadn't realized we had been walking right down the center aisle. "Let's sit here," Chigger said pointing into the second row. "Front row's too close for me. I can't believe some dummies sit up there. Gives me a crook in the neck staring up at the screen."

Although I couldn't see a bit of difference between the first ten rows except that Mom always said, "You'll ruin your eyes sitting that close to the screen," I hunched down in the seat bracing myself like I was about to go down the roller coaster at the Brown County Fair. I didn't mind the cartoon, but from the opening scene of that movie parts of bodies flew every which way. The movie had to do with a crazed scientist with a dark complexion and a foreign accent trying to take over the world by reviving corpses, which then went berserk. The corpses were indestructible and they were jealous of people who were still alive, like us. In some ways the zombies reminded me of Henry. After the first couple of minutes I didn't notice much of the movie, except what I could hear, because my eyes were clamped shut.

Occasionally Chigger glanced sideways at me to ask, "What's the matter with you?"

"Got some popcorn in my eye."

"Lemme see."

"It's all right now."

Chigger sighed. "Sheez. What a baby."

Luckily, she became so absorbed in the movie, her mouth hung open, her eyes glued to the screen, that she soon left me alone.

Throughout the theater, kids shrieked in

delicious terror. With my eyes closed my imagination went wild, which I think was even worse than the movie itself. I tried to cover my ears, too. Sometimes I peeked at the screen and was relieved to see only a handful of screaming people being carried away to the mad scientist's laboratory.

Several years later when the movie finally ended I sagged in my seat, just as Chigger sat bolt upright and protested, "It can't be over yet. It *can't* be. It ain't fair!"

I sighed. "Yeah, that's too bad."

She looked suspiciously at me; then her eyes began to shine. "Hey, let's watch it again!"

I could almost feel my hair turning white, until I remembered. "They clear the theater after every show."

Chigger kicked the seat in front of her, causing the fat guy sitting in it to growl at her. Ignoring him, she brightened with an idea. "We can pay again! It's worth it, ain't it?"

"I don't know. It's a pretty expensive movie."

"What do you mean? It only costs a quarter— two bits. You can't get kicks cheaper than that."

I was shocked, thinking that maybe I'd better join the summer reading program at the library like Henry. Then I realized in delight, "I don't have any more money. How about you?"

"Oh, sure!"

"You do?" I rose from my seat. "I gotta go pee again."

Chigger dug into her pockets, but only came up with seven cents. "Where'd it all go to?" She glanced down at the remains of the snacks from the concessions counter. "If only I hadn't of ate all that stuff."

After I had gone to the restroom again, Chigger and I walked out into the bright June afternoon. As usual, she was talking a mile a minute. "Man, that was great, wasn't it, Luke? I still got goose bumps!"

"Me, too," I said, and I wasn't lying, at least about the goose bumps.

"Wasn't that just about the greatest movie in the world?"

"Sure." I staggered through the blinding light. "But not as good as *The Blob*."

"'Course not. No movie's that good. But we still got to go back again soon as we get some more money. Maybe we can find us some pop bottles to return for the deposit. You know, it all seemed so *real*. 'Specially when that scientist started to eat his assistant."

I started burping Milk Duds.

"I never seen so many bloody arms and legs flyin' around at one time."

I tried hard to think of happy thoughts like about Christmas, but it was six months away.

"And wasn't that great when that blood started squirtin' out of that guy's head just like a lawn sprinkler! Hey, what's the matter with you?"

"Nothing."

"You shouldn't've ate so much."

"*Me* eat too much? What about you?"

"I'm a growing girl. Leastways that's what my mom says. Besides, my *metabullism*, or whatever that's called, is set a little high, like I'm always in overdrive."

I was surprised that she'd ever given that much thought to herself. I wanted to talk more, to learn more about her, mainly why she and her mother had come to Roscoe. But we ran smack into Buzz, Gilman, and Toby in front of the Roscoe Cigar Store and Fountain. They backed away from me like I had a rare tropical disease.

Buzz shook his head. "What a stupe, Zielinski.

You'll never learn, will you?"

For some reason Chigger remained a lady; that is, she kept her mouth shut.

"You're not gonna have any fun this summer," Gilman told me.

I stood there, hands at my sides.

For three years we had squabbled, name-called, and fought, but through it all we had remained buddies. "Well, you started it, Buzz," I said. "And I won. Fair and square."

"That ain't it," said Toby.

"It's her." Buzz nodded to Chigger. "We don't hang around with people who've got cooties."

"Yeah, we ought to've named her Cootie instead of Chigger," said Gilman, grinning with his mouth hanging open like a shaggy mutt.

"She oughta have been in that movie. She could've been the star," said Toby.

Her green eyes softening, Chigger said, "Go ahead and say what you want. Luke here will stick up for me. He's real brave." I couldn't believe what she was saying, especially as I kept having flashbacks from the movie.

Toby swung around a parking meter, Gilman began to whistle like he was real cool, and Buzz just shook his head. "Come on, guys, let's get us a cherry Coke."

"Who needs them?" Chigger said as the guys strolled into the Cigar Store and Fountain, the glass door swinging shut behind them. She turned to me. "They're just being stupid."

"With a capital *S*," I said, copying the phrase from Mom.

"Come on!" Chigger said. "We'll have a lot of fun

this summer by ourselves, won't we, Luke?"

Having nowhere else to go we strolled back toward my house and I asked, "Where'd you say you came from?"

"You mean last?"

"Yeah."

"Indianapolis."

As I knew from living in Tacoma and visiting relatives in Chicago, you could easily get lost in a big city. If you didn't like some friends, you could always look for others. What Chigger didn't understand was that there weren't many choices for friends in Roscoe.

"Why'd you come here?" I asked her.

She shrugged. "My mom heard they was hiring at the shirt factory." She must not have liked the way I was looking at her because she snarled, "What business is it of yours what me and my mom do? She got work. That's what counts." Brightening, like she was making herself be happy, she asked, "What about you? You ain't from around here, are you?"

I wanted to know a whole lot more about her, but for the time being I told her, "No, we moved here three years ago. I've lived lots of places—Illinois, Montana, Washington State. My dad's in the Air Force."

"Man, you've moved almost as much as me!" she said. "'Course all of mine have been in Indiana."

I was amazed that anybody could have moved more than us, especially if they had any choice in the matter. I thought of Dad saying, "If they try to transfer me again, I may resign. They can't just move a man and his family around so often." I wondered if Chigger and her mother had to move so frequently because of her father, like Mom had said, but I could tell it was a private family matter with her.

Chigger's eyes got soft again. "Sorry about draggin' you to that ol' movie. I should have known people gettin' chopped up would bother you. But you don't have to hang out with me if you don't want to. You can go have fun with them guys instead."

"I'd rather play with you any day," I said, and the funny thing was that I suddenly realized it was true. I did feel sorry for Chigger, even when she got snarly, but she was what my dad called "an individual." She had her faults, but so did I. I was a coward for one thing, and I was so closely looked after by Mom that I admired Chigger's independence as well as her spunk.

"You really like playing with me?" she asked in amazement.

"Yes."

We found ourselves walking along the path, which led through the pasture from her house to mine.

"Hey!" she said, snatching my arm. I immediately glanced around for snakes. But Chigger simply peered at me. Her eyes burned with this strange green light. "I know what we can do! You wanna be blood brothers? Or blood brother and sister or—oh, hell, you know what I mean."

I cringed at the mere thought of pain, but at least she wasn't asking to be my girlfriend, "Uh, yeah, sure, I guess so."

She had a penknife for pricking the tips of our fingers, but when it came right down to it, what with the movie, I'd seen enough blood to last me for more than a while.

"Hey, I've got an idea," I suggested. "Let's just be best friends."

She lit up like the used car lot with its rows of electric bulbs over on the highway. "Okay, we'll be best friends forever and ever!"

    We spat into the palm of each other's left hand and shook on it, which to my relief hardly hurt at all.

VII.

EVER SINCE I'D KNOWN CHIGGER, I'd wanted to explore the neighborhood, looking for her apartment. I always chickened out, though, or else she showed up at my house first. I knew that she didn't want anybody finding out where she lived. But now that we were sort of blood brother and sister I figured that she wouldn't mind, at least not too much.

So, the next morning I decided this would be the day. It was a Thursday, I was fairly sure, since during summer vacation I often lost track of the days. Anyway, I figured I'd get an early start and surprise Chigger before she had a chance to get over to my house. But first I had to get through another of Mom's gargantuan breakfasts. Sitting down at the table, I confronted platters and bowls of scrambled eggs, sausage, oatmeal, biscuits and gravy, and toast.

Will was already drowning his eggs in ketchup and Henry was shoveling sugar into his coffee, most of which was milk. Since she claimed to be a lady, Sis delicately nibbled a corner of her toast, while Greg, as usual, got most of his oatmeal on his face.

I was always amazed that I could get up any kind of appetite, having to eat with the pack of them. But I went ahead and piled some of everything onto my plate, and gulped it down in record time, washing it down with milk and orange juice.

"Where do you think you're going?" Mom asked me as I pushed away from the breakfast table.

Dad glanced up from the newspaper and sipped his coffee.

I stood there wondering how Mom always knew what we kids had up our sleeves. Wiping my hands on my jeans, I mumbled, "I was going over to Chigger's."

Mom and Dad both peered at me, which was never a good sign. Finally Mom said, "I don't think that's such a good idea. You better stay home. There's plenty to do around here."

I should have known that Mom would throw a monkey wrench into my plan. "But Chigger always comes over here and I never get to do anything at her house," I explained.

Mom had to nod in agreement. "That girl spends so much time here that she's just about become a fixture."

Dad chuckled. "I thought you always wanted another daughter, Madge."

"That's exactly what I'm afraid of," Mom said. "The girl hangs around here so much she may as well move in!"

"Well, we do have an extra room," Dad observed.

"Very funny."

"As far as I can see, she's a good kid," he said, finishing his coffee in a single, long swallow.

"That has nothing to do with it," Mom argued. "We don't know anything about her background."

Dad chuckled again. "We probably wouldn't want to know."

"And the way she eats!"

"From what Luke tells me, it is amazing." Crinkles formed around Dad's eyes like they always did when he smiled thinly and recalled something sad. "Sort of like those kids in Korea, only they were everywhere." I remembered his telling me he'd seen kids so hungry that they were eating bits of paper picked out of the garbage cans. He shook his head. "And we're not supposed to have kids going hungry like that in America."

Mom frowned. "I know the girl needs attention, but she's been spending every waking hour with Luke."

"He needs the company," Dad said. "I worry about the boy fraternizing with all those animals."

"They're my pets!" I exclaimed, although I knew he was just kidding me.

Mom said, "Luke might pick up bad habits."

"Yeah, and what about cooties!" hooted Will, just about laughing himself out of his chair.

Dad wiped his mouth with his napkin and shoved away from the table, muttering, "If I don't hurry, I'm going to be late for work. We can talk about this later."

Mom followed him to the door. "Don't get me wrong, Frank. I don't have anything against the girl. It's the way people talk about her. I don't want them to think Luke's 'different,' too."

Dad flared. "Since when have you cared what anybody thought, Madge?"

"Well, it's just that we have to live here."

"So does she."

"But there's something going on with that girl's parents. I can feel it in my bones. It could get dangerous."

They looked at each other a minute; then Dad said, "Don't worry. Luke's a smart kid and these things have a way of working themselves out."

We all said goodbye to Dad; then quietly, almost on tiptoes, I moved toward the door.

"Where are you going?"

"Outside."

"Remember what I told you."

"Aw, Mom."

"It's not that I mean to be hard on the girl, Luke," Mom said as she slid the breakfast dishes into a sink full of sudsy, hot water. "I have your best interests at heart. We don't know anything at all about her family. Here they've been in town going on two months now and her mom hasn't joined any of the clubs. She hardly goes out except to the grocery, and nobody's seen her even once at the beauty parlor."

"I don't understand."

"You will when you're older. Why don't you go over and see Pamela Young," Mom said, "if you want to play with a girl."

I made a sour face. "I don't want to play with girls exactly. It's just that it isn't fair *not* to play with Chigger."

"It's only a precaution," Mom said. "We can't do anything about her coming over here, I suppose, but you aren't to go anywhere near her house. There's something brewing over there and I don't want you mixed up in it. Lord knows, I've got enough on my mind without having to worry extra over you. Now go outside and do something constructive with yourself."

Later that morning Chigger came over to my house, as was becoming a habit with her. I was slouched on the porch steps, feeling sorry for myself and mad at the world. Chigger must have picked up on my mood, because she stopped in the yard well away from me.

I immediately asked her, "How come you don't want me to know where you live?"

She blinked twice. "What's this? The sixty-four dollar question?"

"Are you trying to keep people away on purpose?" I asked.

Her eyes narrowed as she stared back at me. "Why would I want to do that?"

"You've never even told me where you live."

"That ain't so."

"Yes, it is."

"It's just that it's, well, it's funner playing over here. That's all."

I eyed Chigger, which prompted her to declare, "Okay, we'll go over there right this very second. If you think it's gonna be so special over at my house, I'll just show you what it's like."

Now it was my turn to squirm like a centipede had crawled down my neck. Thinking about Mom's directive, I said, "You sure your mom won't mind?"

"'Course not, 'long as we don't make too much racket. She's sleeping now on account of she works the second shift, but we can play in the yard. Come on!"

I sat there like I was bolted to the porch steps. "I can't."

"How come? You scared of other people's houses, too?"

I hung my head. "I just can't."

Chigger might have been behind in school, but she seemed to be able to see right through people. She reared up and sputtered, "You mean you ain't allowed to. That's it, ain't it?" My not saying anything must have given her the answer. "Well then, just sneak over. Nobody'd know the difference."

I shook my head. "I would."

"So?"

"It wouldn't be right."

"Look who's talkin' about what's right! Maybe people shouldn't sneak around, but they shouldn't be so uppity either."

"I'm not uppity."

"Yes, you are, and so's your mom. I know she hates my guts."

"No, she doesn't, at least not exactly," I said.

"Yes, she does too hate my guts," Chigger said, glancing down at each of the big toes that were peeking out of the holes in her sneakers.

"Mom acts like she doesn't like anybody," I explained. "But on the inside she's as soft as vanilla pudding. Besides, she just doesn't know much about you and your family, and doesn't know what to think."

"Ain't nothin' to know about my family," Chigger claimed, holding her ground out there in the yard.

Although the only family problems I ever had were Henry and Will, I knew that Chigger was having some kind of trouble at home, which I couldn't quite figure out. "Come on, Chigger," I said. "You can tell me."

She must have seen the concern in my eyes because she admitted in a hushed tone, "Me and Mom got to lay low, so nothin' bad won't happen to us."

My stomach doing flips, I said, "Roscoe's perfectly safe. People around here won't do anything more than annoy you."

"But that don't stop other people from coming here. It's a free country, you know." Her green eyes seemed bottomless as she gazed at me. For once she didn't seem to have anything else to say.

Although I had a pretty good idea who she was talking about, quiet as my own breath, I asked, "Is it your dad? Is that how come he doesn't live at your house?"

She hitched up her nose. "I'd say that twern't none of your business."

"Maybe you're right," I said, ashamed of myself for being such a nosy busybody. "But I'd still like to know."

"I don't want to talk about him."

"Why not?"

"Just say he's worse than that scary movie we saw yesterday."

"What do you mean?"

"He's *real*," Chigger said. "Don't you know the difference between what's made up and what's real?" We faced each other for a while, not saying anything. Could the gossip in Roscoe be right for once? Was he really dangerous? As far as I was concerned I had the greatest dad in the world. I couldn't even imagine having to hide from your own father.

"People are always wanting to know too much about me, Luke," Chigger explained, squishing her hands together like she was trying to tie knots in her fingers. "What I need is for you to be my friend and *not* ask any questions."

It was like she was ashamed of her father, like she was the one who'd done something wrong. "It's not your fault," I said.

"Well, it ain't nothin' to feel good about either, is it? You know, people treat me like I'm too weird for words. And they treat Mom the same way, too. We can't help it if we ain't like everybody else around here."

"You're as good as anybody," I said. "And I like hanging out with you."

Chigger brightened. "Really?"

"Sure!" I said. "You can maybe become an honorary member of our family, you know, like on the Mickey Mouse Club."

The way I figured it, I had more than enough family and Chigger maybe needed a little more. But, come to think of it, I didn't want to have a thing to do with my own brothers and sister, and we all steered clear of Mom. So Chigger and I ended up just playing by ourselves like we usually did.

We went out to the backyard and took the baby bunnies out of the hutch and messed around with them. They were five weeks old, just about the length of time I'd known Chigger, and big enough that they could be handled without Sugar getting too riled.

Lying there in the shade, watching the bunnies hop around in the cool grass, I felt especially good. So I asked Chigger, "You want to have lunch with us today?"

"Lunch?" she asked, like she'd never heard the word before.

"Yeah."

"Well, I don't know."

"The food's good," I assured her, although, thinking of my siblings, I couldn't say much for the company.

"You sure it'd be okay?" she asked.

"Sure," I said, figuring if I wasn't allowed to go over to Chigger's apartment, I could at least bring her more deeply into our home.

We put the bunnies back into their hutch and went into the house through the backdoor, which led directly into the kitchen.

Mom was pulling a macaroni and cheese casserole

out of the oven.

From across the expanse of linoleum I asked, "Chigger can have lunch with us today, can't she, Mom?"

Mom could hardly say no, I thought, especially with Chigger standing right there in the doorway. Placing the casserole on hot pads on the table and keeping her back to us, she said, "I don't think so, Luke. Her mom probably expects her home."

"But—"

Mom gave me "the look," which shut me up quick.

As I backed out of the kitchen, I couldn't have felt more awful. I didn't know what to say to Chigger, which didn't matter, because when I glanced to the screen door she had vanished. I looked for her in the yard, but she must have run home and I couldn't even go after her.

I could hardly eat any lunch that day, even though I loved that gooey orange casserole. I kept hoping Chigger would come back, but she didn't.

All afternoon I moped around the house. Usually, I liked being by myself, but that day, hearing the squeals, whoops, and hollers of the other kids in the neighborhood, always at a distance, was pure torture to me.

"You ought to get out and play with your friends," Mom urged as she lugged the laundry hamper down the stairs. "You've hardly seen Buzz and the guys this summer."

"I'm not getting 'underfoot', am I?" I asked, the tiniest hint of challenge in my voice.

She didn't bother to answer me.

Although Greg and I were the only kids at home,

we were being quiet. Well, at least I was. Greg had this habit of making gigantic structures with his building blocks. Then, backing up to get a running start, he tackled them so that they splattered across the floor with as much noise as possible. It seemed to be his way of making up for not talking much.

"It's not healthy being cooped up in the house during the summer time," Mom called to me as she descended the basement stairs.

Moodily, I wandered outside to visit my rabbits again, although I was actually getting tired of hanging around with animals so much. As I walked across the yard, Gilman rode up on his bike. Stopping in the drive some distance from me, he announced in a formal tone of voice, "Buzz sent me with a message." He dug a scrap of paper out of his shirt pocket and read somewhat jerkily, "Buzz says, uh, 'If you tell Chigger to go jump in a lake right in front of everybody, downtown on the liars' bench, tomorrow, at high noon, we can be friends again.'"

I reminded him, "There aren't any lakes around Roscoe, only the old limestone quarry on the way to Bloomington."

Gilman's mouth dropped open and his eyes got this blank look. "Uh, well, I don't know about that. The quarry might do, but I ain't for certain. I better ask Buzz to make sure."

"Don't bother," I told him, sighing right down to the bottom of my stomach. "I won't tell Chigger to jump in a lake or a quarry or anything else."

"How 'bout the river?" Gilman asked hopefully. "It's good and muddy. Buzz would probably like that."

"No deal," I said.

"It's your life," he said, turning his bike back

down the drive.

I went around for the rest of the day feeling pretty sad about Chigger not coming back, and me not having any other friends in the world. At dinner Henry and Will kidded me more than ever about being such a homebody. The evening did pick up with our outing for ice cream. Will and I were just returning with our delivery when I stopped cold.

Chigger was sitting on our front porch! I was thrilled that she had decided to come back on her own, alive and well. Immediately conscious of my good manners, I realized that she was our guest and that we didn't have an ice cream cone for her.

"Hi," I told Chigger.

She echoed, "Hi."

The formalities taken care of, I announced, "I've got a stomach ache," which was sort of true, because I'd been so worried about hurting Chigger's feelings. I handed my ice cream cone to her. "Better eat it fast before it melts."

"I ain't hungry," she said.

I knew better than that. "Go ahead. Eat it."

"Thanks." She looked gravely at me before turning her full attention to the ice cream.

Sis looked around and said, "Now Luke doesn't have any, Mom."

Henry read on, smiling into the pages as he turned them, and Will sniggered at me.

"Luke has a guest," Mom explained, glancing darkly at Chigger.

We were all silent for a moment. Then Dad breathed a great sigh and pronounced, "I knew I shouldn't have had that second helping at dinner. I can't eat another bite. Here, Luke, take mine."

"I'm really not hungry," I said, but Dad insisted. I knew Mom also would have given me her cone (which would have been quite a sacrifice for her, considering her sweet tooth), if Dad hadn't offered me his, so I needn't have felt like such a hero.

Glancing at Chigger, who had already devoured her ice cream cone, Dad remarked, "Whew, girl, you sure put that away fast."

Chigger looked shyly at the floorboards, painted grey like they were on every porch in Roscoe, and shrugged. "Guess I was a little bit hungry after all."

Dad chuckled. "I'd like to see you when you're *a lot* hungry."

The rest of us had barely gotten a start on our cones and, like Mom said, we were no slouches when it came to ice cream, especially in warm weather when, if you didn't eat fast, it tended to work its way down your arm.

Dad tousled Chigger's hair. "You'll have to come over more often, young lady."

"Yes, sir," answered Chigger, still not looking directly at him.

"Where have you been hiding your friend, Luke?" Dad asked me.

I shrugged. At least he wasn't referring to her as my girlfriend, like he had the other day.

"You know, we have ice cream most every night during the summer," he said to Chigger. "It's a family tradition."

"Yes, sir," she said, standing practically at attention, her arms flattened against her sides.

With his humor and his generous spirit Dad readily made Chigger welcome in our home. Mom still didn't like having her around, but the next evening eight ice cream cones were ordered, helping Will to balance the tray, because thereafter Chigger never missed a night.

VIII.

A FEW DAYS LATER IT GOT HOT, the first really hot day of the summer. Just after lunch Mom gazed out the kitchen window and observed, "Hot enough to fry an egg on the sidewalk."

Will, Sis, Greg, and I perked up. Even Henry looked up from his book, the ninth since breakfast.

Throughout the year Mom cleaned house non-stop. As much as she complained about the work, she wasn't happy unless thoroughly occupied. Yet, come hot weather, her mood improved considerably, to the point where she couldn't resist the municipal swimming pool over in Garfield Park.

"I've got our season pass to the pool," she told us, as if she were letting us in on some deep secret. Of course, we already knew, just as every year we knew where she hid the Christmas presents. "Do you kids feel like a swim today?" she asked, like it was a little private sin instead of a simple treat.

Suddenly we were all whooping, laughing, and dancing jigs.

Other kids had been at the pool since Memorial Day, no matter what the temperature, but Mom always waited until the really hot weather set in. Retiring to the bedroom, she changed into her bathing suit, the material for which Dad claimed she had gotten at Roscoe Tent and Awning.

Henry, Will, Greg, and I rushed to our rooms, pulled on our striped boxer-style trunks, with the tie string in front so we wouldn't lose them off the high-dive, and then tore back downstairs in record time. Elbowing each other, we piled into the car and immediately screamed back toward the house, "Come on, Sis!" "Hurry up, Sis!" "Get a move on it!" until our kid sister appeared in her rose and white polka dot suit. She paused on the porch, as if striking a pose as Little Miss America; then strolled over to us and finally climbed into the car in extra slow motion to further infuriate my brothers and me.

Mom could always be counted on to bring a towel for each of us, as well as suntan lotion, the season pass, and spare change for our traditional stop afterwards.

Sitting in the backseat, I squirmed with delight, not only because we were going to the pool, but also because I was hoping that we might include Chigger.

The moment she got behind the wheel of the car I asked from the back seat, "Mom?"

She acted like she hadn't heard me.

"Mom?"

She sighed. "Yes, Luke."

"What about Chigger?"

Mom ground the gears and her teeth at the same time. The car lurched forward a few feet, then stalled. Staring straight ahead, Mom kneaded the steering wheel and remarked, "Somehow, Luke, I knew you were going to ask about her."

"Well, she might like to go swimming with us."

Will and Henry groaned. Sis held her nose. "P-U."

Ignoring them, I addressed myself to Mom, "Please?"

She drew a long breath. "Do you know where she lives?"

I spoke like an authority. "Over by Old Man...I mean...over by Mr. Bradley's key shop. She and her mom have an apartment."

"Apartment?" Sis asked as, letting go a long sigh, Mom pulled down the drive.

"Yes," I said importantly. "And I bet you a million dollars you don't know what an apartment is."

"I do, too," claimed Sis, her nose stuck up in the air.

"What is it then?" Henry asked her.

Sis leaned over and whispered to Mom, "What's an apartment?" When Mom didn't answer her, she glanced around the passing scenery for a clue; then declared, "It's a doghouse."

Henry guffawed. "Yeah, that's what it is."

"It is not!" I shot back.

"Well, it is sort of. It's where people who are too poor to have a house live," Henry said. "It's like living in a trailer."

Suddenly Henry and I were wrestling over the back of the seat.

"Boys!"

Glaring at each other, we separated and I thought of how much better I liked Henry when he had his face stuck in a book. Maybe I could talk the public library into having a winter reading program, too.

We were in the vicinity of Chigger's apartment now. Leaning forward and peering out the window, I said, "I think it could be that house—or maybe that one. It's a white house. That's what Chigger told me."

"Luke," Mom sighed. "Most every house in Roscoe is white."

We were just about to give up when I noticed Chigger ambling down a set of stairs on the outside of a house near the corner. She was looking at her feet, and I smiled to see her as preoccupied as I usually was. I shouted out the back window, "Hey, Chig! Wanna go swimming?" She looked shocked to see us there, like she'd been caught somewhere she wasn't supposed to be. "Come on, get your bathing suit!"

Without a word, she turned and fled back up the stairs and into the house.

Henry griped. "What's she doing?"

"Maybe we better go on," Mom said to me.

"Wait a second," I said.

Licking my lips, I studied the white clapboard house, which was not unlike other houses in Roscoe except that the stairway zigzagged up its side to Chigger's apartment, which had its shades drawn.

"She's never coming out," Henry groaned. "We'll never get to the pool. She's just hiding in there."

"Maybe I should go in," I said, although something about that apartment gave me the creeps— worse than that scary movie. Then Chigger popped out the door with a little pink and lavender bundle.

"It's about time!" Henry groused as she trotted down the stairs.

Without a word Chigger squeezed into the back seat next to me, although Henry had the entire front seat to himself. Twisting around, he boasted to her, "I'm the oldest one in this family. That's how come I get to sit up front."

Chigger screwed up her nose. "So? I'm the oldest *and* the youngest in my family."

Henry sputtered with indignation. "How can you—"

She grinned at him, like she really had him. "'Cuz I'm the onliest."

Henry sank back in front. "I knew that!"

Chigger folded her arms and grinned back at him. "Well then, how come you didn't say so? Huh?"

Wisely, Henry went back to reading his book.

Will and Sis just gawked at Chigger. As usual Greg looked out the window, not bothering much with anybody. Mom often said it was a blessing to have at least one child who wasn't too rowdy, although I always claimed to be well behaved. She asked Chigger, "Did your mother say it was okay for you to go swimming with us?"

"No'm."

"No?"

Chigger shook her head. "I didn't ask her, on account of she's sleeping. But it don't matter. She don't care nohow."

From the way her jaw was working I could tell Mom wasn't exactly impressed by this answer.

We rode along silently for a while; then Will pointed out to Chigger, "You don't have a towel."

"So?"

Henry smirked as he read his book.

But Mom exhaled. "I brought an extra towel."

It was like she knew all along that Chigger was coming with us. I smiled to myself and tried to find Mom's eyes in the rear view mirror, but she was looking straight ahead, down the road, like she always did when she was being softhearted and didn't want anybody to know about it.

When we got to the pool I hesitated. Our season

ticket was for the family, which meant it shouldn't include Chigger. We'd have to pay an extra fifteen cents for her as a guest. Mom ground her teeth like she always did when she was deciding to do what other people might think was wrong; then she flashed our family season pass.

The man at the gate chuckled, "All of these belong to you, lady?"

Mom glanced over the assemblage of towheads, and Chigger with her distinctly brown hair, and declared, "Yes, they do."

"Her, too?"

"Certainly," Mom said in that tone which meant she didn't want to hear another word about it.

The man laughed, "Well, you're sure getting your money's worth."

I knew that Mom wasn't trying to cheat the park district out of fifteen cents. It had been her hearing about Chigger's mom not caring what she did. Nothing brought out the good side in Mom more than neglected children. However, she was as honest as Abe Lincoln. Still grinding her teeth, she excused the criminal act and the white lie by mumbling to herself, "She may not be my child, but she certainly spends enough time at our house to qualify."

This gesture was not lost on Chigger, who stared up at Mom as though she was a monument, big as the Warner Building downtown, made all the more awesome by her unexpected kindness. At that moment I was as proud of Mom as I was of Dad with all his medals.

We passed through the brick bathhouse, which had a curved tile roof like a pagoda. It was divided into two identical halves—boys to the left, girls to the right.

Sometimes we had to get a basket for our clothes and a safety pin with a number on it, but most often we felt smart because we had changed at home and could just breeze through the room, wading through the splash pool to kill any itchy fungus growing between our toes.

Older guys bragged about peeking into the girl's locker room, but for the life of me, I had never been able to figure out why they would want to do so. This summer, however, I was beginning to feel a strange urge, a blend of curiosity and deep feelings, although I still wasn't sure why. It was like my body and mind weren't getting along with each other anymore.

"Wait for Chigger," Mom told us.

"Aw, Mom," Henry moaned, "Why do we have to wait for her?"

"She's our guest."

"The dumbbell should have dressed at home."

"She didn't have time," I argued.

"She's Luke's guest!" Henry claimed. "Not ours!"

My jerk of a brother had a point there so Mom allowed everyone, except me, to go ahead, cautioning Sis, "Don't go in any deeper than your mosquito bites."

As I stood at the edge of the water I recalled a dream I had once had about the municipal pool, in which I was extremely thirsty. Although there was water everywhere, I couldn't drink any of it, not only because it was chlorinated, but because I suspected that at one time or another every kid in Roscoe had peed in it.

"Last one off the high dive is a rotten egg!" Will hollered as he headed toward the ladder.

The pool was the bulls-eye in Garfield Park, which was the main target of summer recreation in Roscoe, and going off the high dive was the ultimate thrill to everybody—except me, of course. Will loved it and made fun of me, claiming to have been the first of us to learn to swim and the first to jump off the high dive. He now made a career of it, while I could see no point in breaking my neck unless it was for a good cause, like saving a busload of little kids and being a hero and getting a medal from President Eisenhower.

Henry swam the length of the pool; then he went over to the lawn chairs to read again, complaining that he had gotten behind with all the "stupid waiting" for Chigger. Mom took Greg down to the wading pool where she could sit in a webbed lounge chair and keep an eye on him. Despite the heat and her love of the municipal pool, she hardly ever went into the water.

While I waited like a gentleman for Chigger, I glanced around for Buzz and the other guys. Half of my class was there, including Pamela Young, but not those three yahoos, which made me feel good, which made me feel bad because I knew I shouldn't care what they thought of Chigger and me together.

When she appeared at my side Chigger had on a rose and lavender suit with a frilly little skirt around the hips which made her look amazingly like a girl.

Mouth hanging open as he passed us on his second trip to the high-dive, Will said, "She doesn't look too bad in a swim suit. Almost like a normal person." Chigger certainly didn't look any more ridiculous than the rest of us in our suits—stripes, solids, and polka dots—all of which for the sake of modesty were as baggy as could be. Will added, "She doesn't look much different than Sis."

Chigger squinted at him. "So?"

"So," Will joked. "Sis is a girl almost for sure."

But Chigger seemed most concerned about my

opinion. "Don't you laugh," she warned, her fists closing. "Don't you dare laugh at me."

I stammered, "I wasn't."

"Yes, you were!"

"No, you really, you look, uh, kind of pretty."

I had never seen someone's face turn to sunshine so fast. Suddenly I was looking at my feet, which seemed much larger without shoes. We stood there, feeling all gooey inside, and I didn't know what to say next. Luckily, cannon-balling off the high dive, Will splashed us.

Chigger shook her fist at him and growled, "How'd you like a knuckle sandwich."

"Better get in the water while there's still room," I said.

The place was already crowded. "Standing room only," Dad joked on those few occasions he was able to come to the pool with us.

Chigger crept to the edge of the pool and cautiously swished her foot in the water.

"What do you want to do?" I asked.

"Let's go off the high dive."

I just knew she was going to say that.

"Ladies first," I said, a big knot in my stomach.

"I didn't say we had to right now."

I could not have been more relieved.

For a while Chigger and I splashed and kicked around with scarcely a word passing between us. I supposed that she was a little embarrassed by her swimming suit. Every once in a while we looked into each other's eyes in the turquoise water.

"You ain't makin' fun of me, are you?" she asked.

"No."

"Better not be."

However, there was something funny about the way she tilted her head up, like she didn't want to get even a drop of water on her face. I supposed that was why she waded around no deeper than her own mosquito bites. She studied me, then as if to seal our friendship through a secret, she said, "You were real nice to ask me here today, Luke. So, tomorrow I'm gonna show you something."

"What?" I asked, short of breath. Despite my persistent denials of interest in girls, I found that I was curious about her.

"I'll show you tomorrow. I can't show you here."

"Of course not!" I sputtered. "Just tell me. What is it?"

When we were little kids, Mom just threw all of us in the bathtub together, even Sis, which hadn't been any big deal. So I didn't know why I was getting so anxious about what Chigger was going to show me, especially since she was as flat-chested and knobby-kneed as can be.

"I said tomorrow!"

I swallowed. "At least give me a clue."

"Well, okay." She glanced around for eavesdroppers, then got bright-eyed and announced, "Chickens!"

"Chickens?" I'd heard private parts called a lot of different things, but chickens?

"Yeah, chickens," Chigger burst out. "Live ones!"

"What are you talking about?"

"I know how you're all crazy about animals," she explained. "So, tomorrow I'm gonna show you some chickens. What did you think I was talking about?"

"Nothing!" I said, the word rushing out of me along with a sigh of relief.

Chigger eyed me. "You know, you sure can be weird sometimes."

I couldn't disagree with her.

We paddled around for a while, neither of us mentioning the high dive off of which, legs wiggling, Will jumped again and again, blasting the water about as gracefully as a bag of cement.

Gradually the sun swung in an arc toward the ragged line of trees on the west side of the park. I was always aware of the movement of light across the sky and the way shadows shifted. Soon we would have to go home. I didn't know why Chigger hadn't gone off the high-dive yet, but I sure wasn't going to bring up the subject.

Then Buzz, Toby, and Gilman showed up at the pool.

Chigger climbed out of the water and walked along the edge to the deep end to get away from them.

"You look like a slimy fish!" Toby yelled after her.

Whirling around, Chigger snapped, "Look who's talkin'. Blubber Boy himself!"

Everybody laughed, except Toby, of course. Thereafter, he got very quiet.

"And you look like a cross-eyed bullfrog!" she told Buzz.

He yelled back, "Why don't you just get out of *our* pool? You're gonna pollute the water."

"Oh, yeah? Who says it's your pool?"

Just then up on the high dive, Will hollered, "Yippee-i-o-ki-ay!" and sprang off the board, barely avoiding a belly flop.

"You stink," Buzz told him.

"You think you can do any better?" Will demanded.

"Of course, I can, but what I want to see is *her*."

Chigger put on her tough-kid face. "Why should I?"

"To show you're not yellow," Gilman said.

"Divin' off that ol' board ain't nothin'. I could go off it backwards, hopping on one foot, with my eyes closed, and both hands tied behind my back!"

"Let's see you then!"

"Any day of the week."

"How 'bout today, right this very second? I dare you."

"And I double dare ya!" Gilman added.

Chigger drew a long breath, clenched her fists, stomped to the high-dive, and climbed the ladder to the platform, where she stopped dead in her tracks. As she peered down at the water, her eyes widened.

"Do a jack knife!" Buzz shouted up to her.

"Swan dive," Gilman suggested.

"Don't you mean a duck dive?" Buzz laughed. "Quack, quack!"

For safety's sake I wanted to suggest an easy cannonball because Chigger didn't look at all sure of herself, not like when she was up in the sycamore tree. She crept to the end of the diving board, stiffened, panicked, almost lost her balance, and then scurried back to the platform.

"She's scared!" Will said, eyes widening.

Toby and Gilman doubled over with laughter. Buzz yelled, "Watch that first step, girl!"

"You don't have to show off to anyone," I called

up to Chigger, but she was so upset she didn't even hear me. The string of people behind her were yelling, "Come on! Hurry it up, kid. We ain't got all day."

Buzz cupped his hands around his mouth and shouted, "You got a yellow streak down your back that's a mile wide!"

As she crept out onto the board again, Chigger looked so small, so far away.

She just stood there, staring down at the water, in terror. Finally, she squeezed her eyes shut, pinched her nose, and jumped…feet first. The guys twisted up with laughter, especially when Chigger surfaced sputtering, kicking, and thrashing her arms for all she was worth.

"You made her nervous," I yelled, almost shoving the three of them into the water.

"Come on," I called to Chigger, "let's get out of here."

She slipped under the water again.

Everyone seemed to realize it at once—except the lifeguard. As usual, he was picking at his fingernails. I dove into the water. I had never saved anyone's life before and wasn't the world's greatest swimmer. So, as I swam to her I was relieved to see that Chigger was getting the various parts of her body organized enough to dogpaddle toward me. But then she went under again. I dove down and grabbed her around the waist. Then I kicked upward for all I was worth. We broke the surface and frantically I worked her toward shallow water.

"You okay?" I asked, trembling, short of breath, as our feet touched bottom.

She frantically coughed and wiped water out of her eyes. Once she was certain that she was on solid ground, she got hold of herself and gasped, "Sure, heck, yeah."

Yet the way she was hanging on to me I couldn't have pried her loose, and she kept drawing long breaths, shivering from her very depths, and blinking as though surprised that she was still alive.

She had almost drowned, I thought with a ringing in my ears, my heart still whacking away. However, the point was apparently lost on Buzz, Gilman, and Toby, who strode over to the ladder, shoulders thrown back and chests stuck out, and got in line. When their turns came, Buzz and Gilman dove off the board, looking none too great, but at least they went into the water headfirst and didn't show any fear. When Toby approached the end of the board, it bent way down, and as usual Buzz shouted, "Beached whale!"

To get away from them, Chigger and I went over to the kiddie pool and sat down on towels.

"Them assholes," she said. I knew of no rule against cussing at the pool, but looked around for adults anyway. Chigger tried to knock the water out of her right ear. "What do they think I am—a stupid fish? Guess I'm just not used to this here pool."

I looked hard at her. "Why'd you go off that board when you can't swim?"

"I can swim. Didn't you see me?"

"Maybe you dogpaddled a little bit, but you couldn't swim a single stroke when you went off the diving board, could you? You almost drowned."

"But I had to show them bastards."

Again I looked around for adults. "You almost got yourself killed."

"Well, that's tough toenails now, ain't it?"

"Chigger, don't you ever, ever do that again," I said firmly. After such a close call, I was trembling more than her.

Finally she said, "Tell you the truth, me and the water ain't never got along all that good."

I wondered what she did about baths.

It was getting late and presently I got the signal. Mom called Sis over and told her, "Watch Greg a minute." Then she got up, twisted her suit straight, and daintily approached the edge of the pool. In rubber bathing cap, she raised her bulk on tiptoes and like a walrus flopped into the water.

She swam to the rope dividing the shallow from the deep water and back again, always just once to cool off and wash off the suntan lotion. Then she climbed out and called, "Okay, kids. Time to go!"

We didn't need any more encouragement, because Mom had parked the car on the east side of the park not only to take advantage of the late afternoon shade, but to put us in a bee line with the concession stand on our walk back. We never bothered to get dressed at the pool either, Mom always saying, "You never know what you might pick up in that bathhouse." For the first hundred yards we dripped like teabags, but the sun was on our shoulders. Gradually our skin dried and after a while only our bathing suits remained cold and clammy.

Always in a good mood after a swim and with the prospect of a treat at the end of the day, Mom said, "You kids look like a flock of ducks walking along in your rubber flip-flops."

I wanted to tell someone—an adult—what had happened to Chigger so I positioned myself next to her and said, "Mom, Chigger almost…she almost…."

Mom frowned. "I saw it, Luke—the whole sorry episode. I'd like to wring that Buzz Phillips' neck."

The concession stand was an old brick structure with a pagoda roof like the bathhouse, and doors that opened to counters on all four sides. They sold all kinds of sweets there, but under Mom's expert direction we always got frozen *Zero* or *Polar Bear* candy bars.

"One to a customer," she said, except that Greg could never finish his so Mom always had to help him out. She did this with a zealous sense of responsibility, explaining: "Can't let good food go to waste."

Chigger stood quietly to the side, until Mom asked her, "How about you, Chigger?" It was the first time I'd heard an adult call her by her nickname.

"You mean I can have something, too?"

"Of course," Mom said, laying her hand on Chigger's shoulder. "You can have anything you want, honey."

It was then that I realized that Chigger had finally won Mom's heart.

Chigger smiled up at her. "Well, if it's all right by you, Mrs. Z., I think I'll have me a *Zero* bar."

IX.

"**Oh my God!**" **Mom exclaimed**, scattering the contents of her dustpan across the living room. "You scared the living daylights out of me, girl."

"Yes, ma'am," said Chigger, nose pressed against the screen.

"When are you ever going to learn…."

"I'm sorry. I didn't mean nothin'."

The sunlit dust floating around her, Mom went soft. Ever since witnessing Chigger's desperation on the high-dive, she had taken the girl under her wing. Now she was as over-loved as my brothers, Sis, and me. "That's all right, honey," she said to Chigger. "Just don't stand there. When you come to somebody's house knock right away. Don't even wait a few seconds. Do you understand?"

"Yes, ma'am."

"And don't go peeking into people's houses."

"Well, how'm I supposed to know if anyone's home?"

Mom drew a long breath. "Just—oh, forget it."

Literally watching her step, Chigger entered our house. Mom smiled upon her. "Better yet, in the future don't even bother to knock, Chigger. Just come on in. You spend so much time here, you're like family anyway."

"Yes, ma'am." Chigger's grin was wide as a slice of melon. "Is Luke around?"

Thrilled that Mom was finally allowing Chigger to become an unofficial member of our tribe, I slid down the banister from the second floor landing, announcing, "Here I am!"

"How many times have I told you?" Mom rattled the dust mop at me, which was a mistake, since it released more dust particles into the air. Just a month into summer vacation and she was already threatening, "I'm gonna send all of you to the moon!"

Scooping up his books, his nose still in one of them, Henry headed out the door.

"Where are you going?" Mom asked.

Not even glancing up from the page, Henry said, "Back to the library. Got to tell Mrs. Lovington what's in these books before I forget!"

"Just don't walk into a tree," Mom called after him as Henry tripped on the doorsill. Then she turned back to us. "And as for you two, on my cleaning days children are not to be heard *or* seen."

"Yes, ma'am," Chigger and I answered simultaneously. Wide-eyed, Chigger backed out the door with me following right behind her.

"Don't be late for lunch," Mom called after us, "especially if you want to go swimming this afternoon. You know after eating you've got to wait a good hour before going into the water." I smiled to myself because Chigger was now invited to have lunch with us sometimes. Once she even got to stay for dinner. Mom never said much about it, but I knew that she was trying her best to "put some weight on the girl."

Chigger and I fled across the front porch.

"And," Mom called in urgent afterthought, "don't bring home any more of those—" The screen-door slapped shut behind us and we were out of earshot. Mentally I supplied the missing word "chickens," but legally, officially, we were off the hook, weren't we?

Little did I know when Chigger had mentioned chickens at the swimming pool just two weeks ago that they would take over not only our backyard, but our whole summer vacation. At first we had kept the young chickens in the extra rabbit hutches, but they grew fast and now we were swamped with birds, ranging from day-old chicks to leghorns starting to feather out. Already they were eating me out of my weekly allowance, as well as the change from our ice cream runs, which was only a nickel now that Chigger was coming over every night. But at least they assured me of a lack of funds for scary movies. Other than afternoons at the pool and evenings on the front porch eating ice cream, Chigger and I were dedicating our lives entirely to poultry.

We were pursuing the rescue of the baby chicks with such exhilaration that we had forgotten just about everything else. We didn't have time to be pestered by Buzz and the guys, and most importantly, the chickens had helped us to forget about Chigger's family problems, at least for a while.

Old Mrs. Filbert, the kid-hater next door, had already accused us of being gypsies, which I didn't exactly understand except that it had to do with stealing chickens. She threatened to call the health department, which made Chigger and me think we were going to have to bring the chickens in to Doc Phillips for a physical examination.

Hardly a word passed between us as we climbed on our bikes and pedaled hard down the boulevard under that tunnel of green leaves. Since she didn't have a bike of her own, Chigger was kind of borrowing Sis's old Schwinn, which Sis didn't mind as long as she didn't know about it.

There was not a cloud in the sky. The air was like crystal through which the voices of the other kids in the neighborhood rang clearly. The irises had long since given way to impatiens and marigolds. These were the days I wanted to always remember when I grew up, I told myself. When I went into these moods Chigger just kept her distance from me, like I had a bad case of poison ivy.

We didn't know how or why the blond, fluffy chicks had come to be there. Chigger had just stumbled upon them in the trash barrels behind the main building of the Co-op hatchery, peeping among piles of broken shells.

Since the chicks were in the trash, which made it no different than alley hunting, we didn't think we were doing anything illegal. Still, we cruised quietly around the building. Glancing over our shoulders at the weigh station, in case someone might have spotted us, we parked our bicycles in the shade and slipped up to the barrels on hands and knees.

"Watch out!" Chigger called.

We ducked behind the barrels just as a truck loaded with bags of fertilizer passed by.

"Better hurry," I said.

Chigger produced a brown grocery bag with air holes punched into the sides.

"Hold my legs," I said as I leaned over the lip of the metal barrel. Scooping up two chicks at a time, I carefully placed them in the grocery bag.

"Seven this time!" Chigger said as, straining to

get the top of me out of the barrel, I handed her the bag.

"Gimme a hand, will you?"

"What the heck are you kids doin' out there!" a voice suddenly boomed from inside the building.

Just like that, Chigger let go of my legs. I smashed headfirst into the broken eggshells and bits of yolk at the bottom of the barrel. I got myself right side up just in time to see her putting the bag of chicks in the wire basket on the handlebars. She climbed on the bike and started to pedal furiously, only to catch her cuff on the chain.

A pot-bellied man in green work clothes with the name label *Bob* stitched over his shirt pocket materialized in the doorway. The bill of his Co-op cap cut a diagonal shadow across his face, through which his eyes appeared to be little more than sparks of light. Seeing that I was stuck for the moment, he went after Chigger, grabbing her by the scruff of the neck just as she freed herself from the bicycle chain. He pulled her over toward me.

"Lemme go!" Chigger squawked and kicked at him.

"I will when you kids tell me what you're doing back here."

Trying to maintain a little dignity I climbed out of the barrel, brushing eggshells from my hair and shaking them out of my t-shirt. Chigger was in a state of genuine terror, but convinced that we were doing nothing wrong I looked soberly back at the man.

"You kids could get hurt playing back here. What in the heck are you doing anyways?"

"None of your beeswax!" Chigger snapped.

The man flared. "Then scat! And if I see you hanging around here again I'll call Sheriff Browner!"

Chigger was already halfway back to the bicycles, but standing there trying to keep my legs from giving out under me, I looked him straight in the eye and asked, "What are these chicks doing out here?"

"Chicks?"

"Yeah, what are they doing in the garbage?"

The man's mouth formed a slot, which made him look really stupid; then he lit up. "Oh, I know what you're talking about." He glanced at the grocery bag, then back to me. "You're taking chicks?"

I shuffled my feet. "We're rescuing them."

"Those chicks just didn't hatch," he explained.

Edging back toward us, Chigger sputtered, "Sure looks like they hatched to me!"

The man looked at us as if we were just dumb kids, and chuckled. "But they were late."

Chigger and I looked at each other.

"Come on, I'll show you the operation."

I'd been taught never to trust strangers, but I at least knew his name was Bob and besides I was aching to see the inside of that hatchery.

Bob led us down a hallway into a brightly-lit room with trays upon trays of heated eggs in various stages of development. "You see, we've got it recorded when the eggs in each of these trays will hatch. Hundreds of eggs hatch out at a time, but some just aren't any good and a few are so late they end up being chucked out."

"But those chicks have been dying out there," I said.

He shrugged. "We got too many orders to fill and production quotas to meet. Once this tray hatches out, for example, we ship out the chicks, then turn right around and incubate another set of eggs in it. We ain't got time to mess with a handful of chicks that ain't worth two cents apiece wholesale. Besides, late chicks ain't top quality. We operate on volume here, but you kids wouldn't understand that, would you? We got to have a decent profit margin."

Chigger went limp.

"It all boils down to economics," Bob lectured. "You'll understand that when you're older."

I glared at Bob and hoped that I would never understand him. I asked, "What about the chicks that hatch out there in the trash cans?"

"Help yourselves!" he said. "Of course, I'm not the one in charge here and I guess it is trespassing, but I suppose it'll be all right as long as you keep quiet about it. Heck, take all the chicks you find out there. I don't care!"

Although I'd been taught my manners, I couldn't quite bring myself to thank him.

As Chigger and I turned to leave Bob said, "Hey, you kids raise up those chicks and I bet the Co-op would buy them back from you."

"What for?" I asked, since all the animals in my possession functioned as pets.

Scratching his head, Bob said matter-of-factly, "Most of the chickens we sell out of here end up as fryers."

"Fryers?" asked Chigger, shoulders drooping as she released a long, deep sigh.

"We'll think about it," I told him. As we left, his words were ringing in my ears, "Take all you want. I don't care!" Nobody cared it seemed, except Mrs. Filbert, who yelled at us as we pedaled past with our latest cargo of newborn chicks, "Get rid of those smelly chickens, you hear? I won't have them ruining this neighborhood!"

It always amazed me how quickly the summer slipped away, but this summer was going by particularly fast. For the rest of June and well into July Chigger and I never missed a day at the Co-op hatchery. Despite the threats of Mrs. Filbert, we soon had over a hundred chickens in our backyard. "I'm gonna get a gun!" the old lady yelled from her porch the Saturday morning after the Fourth of July. She was especially hopped up because the night before she had been the favorite target of pranksters celebrating our nation's independence. All night long firecrackers had gone off on her lawn.

"I never realized you were so popular," Dad told the old woman the next day as he helped Chigger and me construct a larger pen with chicken wire stretched between the garage and the walkway to the back-porch.

Looking over the flock, she complained, "There ought to be a law."

Dad grinned. "Well now, there isn't a law, is there, Mrs. Filbert. You've checked with everybody at city hall so many times they head the other way when they see you coming."

"I pay taxes. And I'd like to say I'm entitled to more than a little consideration!"

"We should be angry with you, Mrs. Filbert," Dad said as nicely as he could at that hour, "for attracting so much attention to the neighborhood last night."

She went *humph* and receded into her house, slamming the door behind her.

There was a time when I had liked Mrs. Filbert. Her husband had once kept a garden pond filled with goldfish so fat they seemed to waddle through the water. He'd been the one to get me started on tropical fish, but since his death Mrs. Filbert had become the leading moral authority in Roscoe, at least that's what Dad called her.

In checking the city ordinances she had found that you could keep any animal you wanted as long as it didn't disturb the peace by means of any of the senses, mostly hearing and smell. Having been enacted in 1879, the law stated clear as can be that you could have chickens since, as Dad explained, "Everybody kept a small flock back then, and they probably should now. Of course, they kept them for eggs and I doubt they had this many birds."

I glanced around at the July blizzard of white leghorn chickens and remarked, "Oh, we got room for plenty more."

"You're going to have to do something about them, Luke, and soon!" Dad said. "The roosters are maturing and you can't have a hundred of them going off all at once at four a.m."

I recalled Bob's offer to buy back the chickens. We did have enough "volume," that was for sure, but I didn't have the heart to send them to slaughter. Dad seemed to read my mind. "It's all part of growing up, Luke. Facing the facts of life."

I hung my head. "I know."

"You like fried chicken as well as the next guy, don't you?" he noted.

"But we know these chickens personally," I protested.

Although Chigger never said much about the chicks, she was taking on their rescue as an especially personal mission. I wasn't sure why since I was the one who was so sympathetic about animals, but I think it had to do with the chicks being unwanted, like her.

Unable to find a solution to our population explosion of chickens, we stalled for a few more days, which turned into another week. Then one morning an amazing thing happened. We discovered a four-legged chick, walking on its front legs and carrying a pair of smaller withered legs on its rump.

"It's a miracle!" I exclaimed, showing my Catholic roots.

"That'll show that jerk at the Co-op," Chigger said. "This chicken's gonna make us rich and famous!"

"It'll go in the Ringling Brothers and Barnum & Bailey circus!"

"And what about the Ripley's Believe It Or Not section in the comics!"

Proudly, we ran into the house and announced the news to Mom.

"Don't count your chickens before they're hatched," she cautioned us, smiling slightly to herself.

I was thoroughly perplexed. "What do you mean? This one's already hatched."

Chigger and I were so excited by the four-legged chick that we skipped going to the swimming pool that afternoon. "We can put up posters all over town," she suggested, spreading her arms out wide as if to include the whole world in our big plans. "'The Famous Four-Legged Chicken!' We can charge a nickel to look at it and a dime to touch it with one finger. That way we can pay for the feed and maybe even get enough money to build a real chicken coop—maybe even buy a farm in the country and raise more chickens. It can be like a chicken orphanage."

I was nodding in total agreement, convinced that our problems were over.

"That way we can really show Buzz and those

other dopes!" Chigger rubbed her hands together. "Finally I found a way to show them up."

Although I had no objection to cashing in on our discovery, just so long as it helped other chickens, I wasn't particularly interested in getting even. To change the tone, I suggested, "Let's call the newspaper!"

"Now?"

"Sure!"

Suddenly, Chigger's eyes were lit. "It's happening, ain't it, Luke? For once in our lives we're really gonna be important and famous."

We imagined the whole front-page dedicated to Chigger and me, and our four-legged miracle, including a bunch of photographs of us with the chicken. Most adults would rather keep out of the news, since it dealt with scandal and outrage, at least that's what Mom always said, but to us it was the greatest thing in the world.

"Think we could *really* get in the paper?" Chigger asked hopefully.

"Sure. Dad says they're always desperate for anything to happen in Roscoe. They might do…what did he once call it…a human interest story."

"What's that?"

"I'm not sure, but I think it's a story about people that doesn't have anything to do with war or crime."

"But ours is about a chicken. It don't have nothin' to do with people."

I sighed. "You're right."

Chigger brightened. "But everybody likes animals."

I nodded. "Come to think of it, they do have a lot of animal interest stories, too. You know, about a St. Bernard rescuing someone and talking crows and stuff like that."

So we called the *Daily Independent Gazette*, Chigger and I knocking heads as we tried to listen on the telephone at the same time. I described the chick to a man on the other end—they called him the newsroom editor, whatever that meant—but he seemed to yawn into the phone, then asked, "So what?"

I practically shouted, "What do you mean 'so what'? It's got four legs!"

"Tell you what," he said. "You call me back when that chicken's full grown. Then maybe I'll send somebody out to take a picture of it."

Completely deflated, I was putting down the receiver when the editor asked, "Hey, are you the kids over on Milford Boulevard with that yard-full of chickens?"

"Yes!"

"We've sure had a lot of calls about you—close to fifty so far. People keep wanting us to do an exposé about your chickens."

"Oh, those calls are all from Mrs. Filbert."

"Well, I was just curious. Good luck." Abruptly, he hung up.

"We can still put up posters," Chigger suggested. But the rejection by the newspaper had devastated us. Then everybody got home from the swimming pool and we felt worse because we had wasted the whole afternoon.

Not making us feel any better, Mom commented, "Most people aren't interested in chickens until they're frying size."

"Very funny," I said.

Curly-headed Will rubbed his stomach. "They sure do taste good all brown and crispy."

Henry said, "When they're alive all chickens do is go around stinking."

"Not as much as you do!"

That prompted Henry to chase me around the kitchen table until Mom told us to cut it out if we valued our lives. Then Chigger and I went outside to be miserable with each other for a while.

"If it'll make you feel any better you can have dinner with us tonight, Chigger," Mom called after us.

That did somewhat improve our spirits, especially Chigger, who said, "I'm so hungry I could eat a horse." I thought Mom was going to make another joke about that, but for once she and everybody else left us alone.

That evening at the dinner table, in hopes of stirring up some interest I told Dad about the four-legged chicken.

He grinned. "Are you pulling my leg?"

What's with these adults, I thought, rolling my eyes toward the ceiling.

Chigger insisted earnestly, "No, it's really got four legs! You can count 'em for yourself if you don't believe us."

"Well, okay. We'll have a look at it after we eat."

Delighted to finally have someone interested enough in the chicken to actually look at it we went into the backyard after dinner. In the gathering dusk I peered into the rabbit hutch where we kept all of the day-old chicks.

"Where is it?" I asked.

We looked everywhere, getting more and more desperate. Then, turning white, Chigger gasped. Ducking into the hutch, she removed the trampled body from the far corner. I was on the verge of tears. We'd lost chicks before but....

"You should have told me sooner," Dad said. "We could have fixed up a place for it. Special."

"We just found it this morning," I said.

Chigger and I stood there looking at our feet.

"Better bury it," Dad sighed, putting an end to our hopes for fame and glory.

X.

THE DEATH OF THE FOUR-LEGGED CHICKEN shocked Chigger and me. We had begun the rescue peacefully sunk in the summer shade of our little town. Propelled by our good intentions, we had never imagined anything going so tragically wrong.

The next evening we were sitting on the front porch, feeling sorry for ourselves, when a reporter from the *Daily Independent Gazette* showed up in the yard with a camera and note pad. "You the kids with the four-legged chicken?" he asked.

Narrowing her eyes, Chigger stared hard at him. "We *were*."

"It died," I told him.

"Too bad," he said. "Might have made a good story."

"What do you mean *might of?*" Chigger roared. "It would have made a great story! If you'd gotten here sooner you could've wrote all about it."

"Four-legged chicks aren't really that uncommon," he said smugly.

Chigger exploded, "Oh yeah? Let's see you find one!"

"Whoa there," the reporter said. "It's just that double-yolk eggs sometimes end up like that if one of the chicks dies before hatching. Shoot, I once saw a picture of Siamese-twin chickens."

"Really?" gasped Chigger.

"What I'd really like to do is a little story about you kids," he said.

Chigger's mouth dropped open. "Us?"

"Why?" I asked.

He shrugged. "Might be a good human interest story."

Barely able to contain our excitement, Chigger and I sat down with the reporter on the front porch steps. Henry, Will, and Sis gathered like moths around a light. Dabbing the lead to his tongue, the reporter held his pencil poised over his pad and asked us, "So how did you kids get into the chicken business?"

We told him the whole sad story.

"You mean they were just chucking them out?" he asked, becoming more interested.

Chigger reared up. "You're damn, I mean, darn right!"

He scribbled down the facts. Then, like it wasn't a big deal or anything, he said, "Okay, you wanna stand in the chicken lot over there? I'll take your picture."

"*Our* picture?" There were stars in Chigger's eyes. I was practically breathless. "You…you…you mean you're really going to take *our* picture?"

"Natch," he said, as if it weren't the earth-shaking event that it obviously was.

As if in a dream Chigger and I ambled into the chicken yard. We grinned right up to our ears, standing knee-deep in chickens, the rabbit hutches full of chicks behind us. The instant before the reporter snapped our picture with his Speed Graphic camera, Chigger slipped her hand in mine.

"We're really going to have our picture in the paper?" I asked the reporter, just to be sure.

He shrugged. "It's up to the editor. He calls all the shots, you know. Ha, ha."

I remembered the gruff voice of the editor and tried to pin the reporter down. "When do you think it'll be in the paper?"

"Tomorrow. *If* they decide to use it."

Greg was still too young to appreciate what was going on, but after the reporter left, Henry couldn't concentrate on his book for anything, Will had his lower lip stuck out a full inch, and fluffing her hair Sis said, "Well, I'm gonna be Miss America someday, you just wait and see."

"Who gives a hoot about that?" Chigger told her flat out.

Sticking her nose up, Sis ran to Mom in the house.

Not in the least sympathetic, Chigger and I danced around the yard, singing, "We're gonna be famous!" The more we annoyed my brothers the more we loved it.

To get rid of us Mom finally stuck her head out the kitchen window and told Chigger and me that we could go downtown to further broadcast the news that we ourselves were about to be big news in Roscoe. Unfortunately, late as it was, we weren't able to find any of our classmates—Chigger had been especially interested in rubbing it in to Buzz. In fact, all of Roscoe was closed like a clam for the night. I'd waited for years for a chance to stay out late and was completely disappointed to find that even less happened in Roscoe at night than during the day.

"Well, they'll all know about it tomorrow

anyway," Chigger told me.

"*If* they publish the story and picture," I said.

"'Course they will," she assured me.

Just as we split up, Chigger taking the shortcut through the pasture to her home, she grabbed me by the arm and kissed me, right on the cheek. It would be just like her to ruin a momentous occasion.

I lay awake that night, imagining tomorrow's headline: "Heroic Children Rescue Chickens From Certain Destruction!" Maybe we'd get invited to the White House or, better yet, to Disneyland. We might become Hollywood stars. I might actually meet Annette Funicello. Suddenly, at the thought of Annette, I had an attack of guilt. Maybe it was that stupid kiss. So far Chigger and I had been buddies, like brother and sister, although I didn't particularly get along with my real sister.

I looked out the window into the moon-whitened yard, started counting sheep, which quickly turned into chickens, and the next thing I knew it was morning. I still had chickens on my mind, as did Chigger, because she was already on our front porch.

"It's just after dawn," Mom told us.

At the kitchen table with eggs and a second cup of coffee, Dad kidded, "Couple of early birds, huh?"

I rolled my eyes.

"Have you had any breakfast?" Mom asked Chigger.

"No, ma'am...but...uh...I ain't particularly hungry."

Dad got his crinkly look around the eyes as he looked at her and said, "Sure you aren't hungry."

"Well, sit down anyway, Chigger," Mom said. "You may find room for a little something."

Like me, Chigger wasn't in much of a mood for eggs, but she put down two heaping bowls of corn flakes with banana sliced in it, a couple slices of toast slathered with butter and grape jelly, three strips of bacon, and a large glass of orange juice.

"Good thing you weren't particularly hungry," Dad said. "We would have had to send Luke out for more groceries."

Chigger looked down at her plate. "I must've forgot to eat breakfast this morning."

I stared at her, she being the first person I'd ever known other than Henry, who wasn't quite human, who could out-eat me, and she did it by a mile.

"Why are you kids up and about so early?" Mom asked.

As if you didn't know, I thought. "We're going downtown to the *Daily Independent Gazette* office! Gonna get the first paper off the press!"

Mom and Dad glanced at each other and smiled.

"Well," Dad said, leaning back in his chair, "at this rate you'll be the first ones there."

"We'd better be!" said Chigger as she smeared butter and jelly on yet another piece of toast. I had never seen her so hopped up. "We're gonna be about the most famous people in the whole state of Indiana!"

With all the activity in the kitchen, Henry, Will, and Sis, who wouldn't miss anything for the world, began to trickle one by one down the stairs.

"Today's the day we get to see our picture in the paper," I reminded them.

"So what?" Henry said, making his fish face.

"Well, your picture's not in the paper," I said. "And it never will be."

"Oh, yeah? It will be when I win that stupid reading contest!"

"They're not going to put your picture in the paper," Will told us. "It would scare too many people."

"You probably broke that guy's camera," Henry added.

"All right," Dad cautioned us. "That's enough warfare for one morning."

We all settled down appreciably, except Chigger who was squirming so much she could hardly keep her backside in her chair.

Mom said, "I'll pack you and Chigger a lunch."

"Lunch? Why?" I asked.

"In case you get hungry."

I thought she just meant Chigger, as a joke, but then Dad said, "Don't bother, Madge. Their lunch is on me." He reached into his wallet and handed me a whole dollar, saying, "Why don't you two celebrate with hamburgers at the cafe? Come to think of it, the way Chigger eats, I'd better make that a dollar and a half."

Chigger appeared to be in a state of shock.

I sure enjoyed having that money tucked into my pocket, but not as much as hearing the moans and protests of my brothers and sister. "It ain't fair," Will cried. "They're just a bunch of stupid chickens."

"You kids do something important," Dad said, "and you'll get a bonus, too."

I got tingly all over just thinking that we were doing something "important," and Chigger and I weren't even in sixth grade yet, at least not officially.

I waited for Chigger to eat still another piece of toast, which took about three seconds, then suggested,

"We'd better get going."

"Okie-doke." She grabbed two strips of bacon for the road.

Mom and Dad glanced at each other again, like they had some little secret between them. "Off so soon?" Dad asked.

"We can't wait!" Chigger exclaimed. She folded another slice of toast around the bacon and we headed out the door, leaving Mom and Dad chuckling at each other.

"What do you suppose they meant?" I asked as we cut across the yard. "Do they know something we don't?"

"Adults always act like that," she explained, which somehow made sense to me.

By the time we reached Poplar Street we were jogging and as we rounded the corner we broke into a dead run. Chigger was darned fast that day, and I had one heck of a time keeping up with her. She may even have beaten me, but since we weren't racing, at least officially, I figured it didn't count.

At that hour we were the only people downtown. A soft light lay over Main Street. I asked, "Don't you like the, uh, what do they call that stuff…the atmosphere?"

Chigger scowled. "Don't be a sap. We got more important things to do than get gooey-eyed about the weather. Come on, I got a dime. We can buy a newspaper right out of the machine soon as they put them in."

"Better yet, since we're *in* the paper they might just give us one."

"They ought to—one for each of us. I want my mom to see it."

I paused, that being one of the few times that summer she had mentioned her mom, at least willingly.

She'd become such a fixture at our house that I'd almost forgotten she had any kind of family of her own.

We sat down on the curb and waited for what seemed to be an eternity, as the sun rose over the square tops of the buildings. Gradually, I began to lose heart. I let go a long mournful breath and said, "You know, it may not even be in the paper."

"Don't say that!"

I sighed even deeper. "He may have taken our picture too late to get it in."

"He wouldn't have taken our picture and everything if they couldn't get it in the paper."

"Well, adults do all kinds of things that don't make any sense."

Chigger couldn't disagree with that.

Then we heard a *tap, tap, tap* behind us. An old man in wide suspenders and a green visor that covered all of his head except the bald part on top waved us to the window. "What are you kids doing out here so early?" he asked, his eyes like gelatin behind his thick glasses.

"We're waiting for the paper," I told him.

"It's gonna have our picture in it!" Chigger crowed, as if the entire county should hear about it right then and there.

Speaking through the window, he sounded far away. "Well, you're going to have a long wait. The paper doesn't come out until two o'clock."

Somehow it hadn't occurred to me that the *Daily Independent Gazette* was an afternoon paper. Now I knew why Mom and Dad had glanced at each other and had arranged for our lunch.

Pointing to the sidewalk, hardheaded Chigger declared, "Well, we're gonna wait for it right here!"

Hooking his thumbs in his suspenders, the man told us, "Suit yourselves."

I thought to ask, "Uh, do you know if they're having a picture in today's paper of a couple of kids who look a lot like us?"

He shrugged. "Couldn't say. I don't rightly remember. But tell you what, you kids come back at two o'clock and I'll give you a paper. Won't cost you a red cent."

That made Chigger and me feel a little better. As we went back to the curb I noted the time on the bank clock—ten after seven. Roscoe was just coming to life, although that life didn't amount to much, especially at this hour of the day.

"What'll we do now?" I asked, with my face slumped in my hands.

Chigger remained her stubborn self. "We'll wait. Right here."

However, less than an hour later, we were both as wiggly as worms.

"I can't hardly stand it no more," she said.

"You said it. I'm gonna die from boredom."

"That's not what I mean!" she cried. "Don't you see, Luke, I *got* to get my picture in that newspaper. I just got to!"

If the Woolworth's five and dime hadn't opened at nine, they would have had to haul us away to the nuthouse. We hustled into the store where we visited every section, especially the toy department, and handled everything they'd let us put our hands on. I stood in front of the goldfish tank for what seemed like an hour. We walked back outside into what was fast becoming a hot August day. The bank clock read 9:47.

There were plenty of things to amuse us around

town, but with our minds so much on the newspaper, we couldn't get excited about anything else. We window-shopped up and down Main Street, but soon lost interest, once we'd seen everything for the fourth time. Then Chigger wanted to go into the cafe for a second breakfast, which I could hardly believe. Although I was sorely tempted to eat some more just to pass the time, I refused to spend any of the money Dad had given us until we'd seen the newspaper.

The only consolation of that long morning came around eleven. It was actually eleven-o-nine exactly on the bank clock when Buzz, Toby, and Gilman walked by.

"We're gonna have our pictures and names and everything in the newspaper!" Chigger crowed.

Buzz stood in amazement. "You are not!"

"Yes, we are!"

"That's another whopper," Toby claimed. "Just like that talk about her dad and polar bears."

"Is not."

"Why would they put your picture in the paper?" Gilman asked.

"For saving all those chickens," Chigger told him, rocking back and forth on her heels and whistling a little.

"I don't believe it," Buzz said. "Who gives a hoot about chickens?"

"Seein's believin'," Chigger said. "You just come on back here, oh, say round about two o'clock and take a look at that ol' newspaper."

Buzz went out of his way to act like he couldn't care less, so I knew it must have been really eating him up inside. "What's the big deal about having your picture in the paper anyways?" he demanded.

"The big deal is you're *not* gettin' your picture in the paper is what," Chigger informed him. "So you're *not* gonna be famous like me and Luke."

Buzz shrugged. "Who'd want their picture in that stupid newspaper anyway?" He turned to Gilman and Toby. "You guys wouldn't want your picture in the paper, would you?"

"Heck no."

"Not me."

"You're just sayin' that," Chigger told them.

"Now the *Indianapolis Star,*" Buzz went on, nodding to himself, "that would be a big deal."

Chigger swelled up so much I thought she just might burst into bloom. "Well, I already had my picture in the dumb ol' *Indianapolis Star.* Now I'm gonna have it in this here paper, too. So there!"

"You never had your picture in the *Indianapolis Star!*" Buzz protested. "Unless it was for bein' arrested."

She shuffled a little. "Well, I could've."

Although I didn't want to brag, especially since I wasn't sure it was going to happen, I said, "They did take our picture, and everything."

Toby said to both of us, but mostly to Chigger, "Well, who'd want their picture in any paper that's got *your* picture in it?"

"I already seen your picture," Gilman told her, "at the post office. Wanted Dead or Alive."

Chigger contented herself with sticking her tongue out at them as I grabbed her arm and pulled her across the street to the liars' bench in front of Harold's Barber Shop.

"We'll be back at two to see if you're lying again," Buzz called after us.

Ignoring him, Chigger turned to me. "I really showed them, didn't I?"

"I suppose so, if our picture really is in the paper. If it isn't, we'll never live it down."

For the third time that morning we checked the coin returns on the pop machines outside of Pearson's Grocery, then we returned to the liars' bench in front of the barber shop and watched freight cars being unloaded at the railroad track.

At 12:47 Chigger grabbed her stomach and moaned, "I'm just about fit to die of hunger."

"Let's wait until we get the newspaper. Then we can really celebrate."

"But what if our picture ain't in it?" she asked.

I frowned. "Then Buzz and Gilman and Toby are gonna have a field day, the way you were bragging. Anyway, if our picture's not in the paper, we'll at least have lunch to look forward to."

Chigger thought about that for a while, then said, "You are pretty smart sometimes, Luke, even if you don't have any sense."

"Thanks," I told her, although I wasn't sure why.

Finally, excruciatingly, the hour approached. Not making matters any easier, the last hour or so Chigger had her nose pressed against the window of the *Daily Independent Gazette* office. Inside, the newspaper people pointed to her and kidded among themselves, but she was not in the least deterred.

I told her, "It's impolite to stare through windows. Remember what my mom told you?"

"But this is a public business, ain't it?"

I couldn't disagree with her too much, because for the last ten minutes I did the same thing.

At precisely 2:03 the man in the green visor stepped out of the gloom of the back of the building with a neatly folded copy of the newspaper. We rushed to the door. "Here's your paper, hot off the press. This one's on the house," he said as Chigger grabbed the paper. I thanked him and caught up with her on the sidewalk.

"Wait," I said. "Let's go to the cafe."

Chigger's eyes just about popped out of her head. "What the heck for?"

"We can look at it better there."

"You gotta be kiddin' me. I can't wait another second. I just can't!"

"This is a special event," I said. "We got to do everything right so we can, you know, savor the memory."

She looked at me like I was out of my mind.

We went ahead to the Deluxe Cafe anyway, found a table by the window, and carefully laid the newspaper on the red-checkered tablecloth. Unfolding it, I was disappointed not to immediately see our smiling faces on the front page. They had some picture of President Eisenhower on a golf course.

Kneeling on her chair and leaning over the table, Chigger was bouncing up and down. "Hurry up, Luke! I can't hardly stand it no more!"

I turned the page and we were again disappointed.

"Damn! I mean 'dang'!" Chigger beat the table, rattling the silverware, and causing several people to look at us.

As I turned the pages we became increasingly desperate. Chigger was tearing her paper napkin into shreds. "They gypped us!" she cried. "I knew they would.

They always do that!"

Then, at the bottom of the local section front page we spotted the photograph with a caption, "Chicken à la Kids." There was a short article, about the Co-op dumping chicks and praising us as lovers of animals, but it was the photograph that really got to us.

Leaving the paper open so we could stare at the picture in reverent silence, we ordered cheeseburgers, French fries, chocolate malts, and Cokes, after which Chigger had to have a wedge of banana cream pie, which she couldn't finish after all so I had to help her. To my horror our check came to $1.73 with tax, but Mrs. Wilfred said, "Just forget it, kids. Lunch is on me since you're so famous, and such heroes to boot."

Chigger just about blushed her heart out.

Before we went home that day we bought fifteen more newspapers, spending every cent Dad had given us. Chigger said, "I'm gonna plaster 'em up all over my room. Wait'll my mom sees these!"

I was hoping for a parade, a meeting with the Mayor in which we would receive the keys to the city, and a press conference in which we would discuss our role in saving the chickens. Chigger only said, "We done it, Luke. You may not understand this, but I'm finally somebody in this here town."

The morning had gone so slowly, but for half the afternoon, Chigger and I sat on the liars' bench looking at the picture of us with the flock of leghorns like a snowstorm around us, quietly holding hands, our faces aglow in the evening light.

XI.

IN THE DAYS FOLLOWING THE NEWSPAPER ARTICLE, Chigger and I were not invited to the White House. We didn't get the keys to the city or even a phone call from the Mayor. In fact, we received just one invitation, and it was one I would never have expected, not in a million years.

Squirming in the doorway to the kitchen, I turned to Mom and said, "Uh, Chigger's mom asked if I could come have lunch with them today."

Mom dropped her washcloth in the sink-full of grey dishwater. Turning to face me, she asked, "When did this come up?"

I shrugged. "Chigger just asked me this morning. Without any warning or anything."

"Her mother asked you out of the blue, after you've been running around with her all summer long?" Mom said.

"I think it's because we got our picture in the paper," I said. I was dying to see the inside of Chigger's apartment and to learn how she lived. But I was also scared of what I might find there.

Sitting at the kitchen table, Will grabbed his throat, made gagging noises, and pronounced: "You're going to her house? Yuck! You'll probably get warts just from being there."

As much as she had come to like Chigger, I could tell Mom wasn't exactly enthused about the invitation. She asked, "What does Mrs. Chigger—I mean Mrs. Heck—plan to feed you?"

"I don't know."

Mom was a strong advocate of wholesome, home-cooked meals and I knew this question would concern her deeply. Shaking her head, she said, "I don't think your going over there is such a good idea."

"But she invited me. I can't hardly say no, not without a reason."

"How 'bout ptomaine poisoning?" said Henry, slumped into a chair with another book. I'd seen him with so many of them that summer they seemed to be growing out of his hands.

Mom frowned. "Lord knows the girl's spent enough time over here. It's about time she reciprocated."

"Yes, ma'am," I agreed, itching to look up the word.

Mom returned to her dishes for what seemed an eternity; then she sighed. "Well, all right, you can have lunch with her. Just don't eat anything you shouldn't."

"Like what?"

She shrugged. "Anything out of the ordinary."

I had no idea what she was talking about, but began to worry that Chigger's mom would serve me something I wouldn't be able to identify and I'd eat it out of politeness and I'd wake up in the hospital.

I eased out the kitchen doorway.

"Remember to mind your manners, young man!" Mom called after me.

"Yes, ma'am."

After I'd looked up "reciprocate" in the dictionary, I took the shortcut through the pasture, surprised at how Chigger had worn down the grass over the course of the summer, making a clear path from her home to ours. But now I was going in the other direction. I kept telling myself, "There's nothing to be scared about. Chigger comes out of that apartment alive 'most every day."

She was playing in the yard, banging a rubber ball against the garage door. I tried to see if she was as nervous about this visit as I was, but if she was she didn't show it. We climbed the narrow flight of outside stairs and entered a group of rooms on the second floor. The place had a cigarette smell that bit at my nose, like the officers' club at the air base, but more closed up. Yet even if the place had had more windows, I felt that these rooms would still be too dim.

"This here's Luke. And this here is my mom," Chigger said by way of introducing us, flapping her arm at me and then at her mom.

I half-bowed. "Pleased to meet you, Mrs. Heck."

She offered me a sliver of a smile. "Now ain't you sweet?"

It was funny how she looked just like Chigger with the same green eyes and chopped-off hair, except that she was so pale. She had a sad face, like she was about to apologize for something, and crinkles around her eyes like Dad, only hers bent downward.

Her hands kept fiddling with a cigarette as if she couldn't let go of it for the life of her.

"I'm pleased to meet you, Luke," she said, "and welcome to our home. I've heard so much about you from Eddie that I wanted to see for myself what company my daughter was keeping."

I'd forgotten that Chigger had another name. I just stood there, arms dangling at my sides.

"I hardly knew my girl had such a good friend until she showed me that picture in the newspaper. I'm sure proud of you kids. Here I am twenty-eight years old and ain't even come close to having my picture in the paper."

I gulped out a "thank you."

"So, you live in that big white house over on Milford Boulevard?" she said, probably to get me talking, since I'd pretty much clammed up on her.

"Yes," I said, seeing myself reflected in Mrs. Heck's eyes. I was just wearing blue jeans and a striped t-shirt, but it seemed to me that I must look squeaky clean and proper compared to Chigger who always had an assortment of patches on the knees and seats of her jeans.

"Well, you been a true-blue friend to my girl," Mrs. Heck said, looking me right in the face, not over my head like lots of adults did. "And for that I'm grateful. Whenever we move I always worry about how she's gonna get along with the other kids. You even give her that cute nickname, did you?"

I opened my mouth to correct her. But, standing behind her mother, Chigger glanced at me and I could see that hurt look in her eyes.

Mrs. Heck's face brightened for a moment. "I'm so truly happy that my baby's made herself a lot of friends here. I'd say Roscoe is just about the nicest place we've ever lived."

Although her face had briefly lighted up, there was still a kind of darkness around Mrs. Heck's eyes that reminded me of bruises. I noticed that she was secretly observing me, not meaning anything by it. It was just the opposite, I think, like she was worried about what I thought of her, which seemed very strange to me. As a kid, I was more accustomed to grownups judging me.

"Lunch is on the table, babe," she told Chigger. "I'm so wore out from standing at that ol' machine all last night that I can't hardly stay on my feet. I'd appreciate it if you'd go ahead and serve yourselves." She then went back to staring into the smoke rising from her cigarette, seeming to lose herself in it.

Chigger and I sat down at a small table in the tiny kitchen at the far end of the living room.

"Isn't this great?" she remarked, digging into a bowl of canned spaghetti and tomato sauce. "Mom got it special for us."

"Sure is."

Slipping carefully into my seat at the table, I sniffed at the off-color stuff. At least I knew what it was, even if I wasn't quite sure what it was made of. Out of politeness I ate every bite, even though it tasted pretty awful—too soft and squishy for me. Not that we had fancy meals at our house, just the opposite. But we hardly ever ate anything out of a can, unless Mom had put it up herself.

Mrs. Heck remained in the living room, on the couch, smoking one cigarette after another.

"Mom don't eat much," Chigger explained, like she could read my mind.

Mrs. Heck looked exhausted, and like she needed a lot of time to herself.

"They work Mom to the bone at that dumb factory," Chigger went on. "Plus she's got to work second shift, from three to midnight. It's the worst shift, she says, 'cuz it cuts into both your day and your night. It don't leave much time to do stuff, except to sit around being tired."

I was very sorry for Mrs. Heck having to work so hard. I also thought of Chigger coming home to an empty house in the afternoons and evenings. What did she have for dinner, other than the occasional meals at our house, the candy bars we got at the concession stand, and the ice cream cones we had every night on our front porch? As if reading my mind again, she said, "Mom's been tryin' to get on first shift so's she'll have more time to spend with me, but she don't have much seniority."

"Oh," I said, making a mental note to look up the word. I knew it had to do with age, but Mrs. Heck didn't look all that old to me.

We had canned fruit cocktail for dessert, then as soon as I could I suggested, "Better get going. It's almost time to leave for the swimming pool."

"But we got Twinkies for dessert, too! Since it's special your being here."

I slid back into my chair. "Great." I did love Twinkies, but wondered what Mom would think of my eating a whole lunch of junk food.

Chigger buzzed around the apartment, not even noticing the gloom, it seemed to me. But I couldn't wait to get out of there, to be back outside where I would appreciate fresh air and open sky more than ever. When we left, I said goodbye to Mrs. Heck who, despite the dark circles under her eyes, seemed too young to be a mother. I thought they were all supposed to be old and fat and wrinkled like Mom. Standing nearly at attention, I told her, "It was real nice meeting you, Mrs. Heck."

"Same here, honey," she said, smiling a fraction. Although she seemed as uncomfortable with my presence there as I did, she added, "Don't be a stranger now, you hear? You and all of Eddie's friends are welcome to visit any time."

Outside Chigger fidgeted all the way back to my house, then, stopping in the pear orchard, she finally asked, "Well, what did you think?"

"About what?"

"My house."

"It was great."

I must not have been very convincing. We walked along silently for a while; then Chigger said, "Guess you ain't used to them kind of eats."

"Oh, no, we have stuff like that all the time."

She eyed me suspiciously. "No, you don't."

I didn't know what to say, even though I knew that my silence insulted her.

Suddenly a shadow was cast over her face. "I thought it might probably be a mistake inviting you over. But Mom still wanted to, and so did I."

"But I really liked visiting your apartment," I insisted. "And I like your mom, Chigger. She's real nice."

As if she hadn't heard me, Chigger said, "I wanted to do something for you for once. You always being so good to me, and all. After we got our picture in the newspaper, Mom said we oughta maybe show some manners and ask you over. We don't get much company at our house, but I'm always talkin' about you to Mom, and I guess she just wanted to look you over for herself. I admit there ain't much to brag about at my place. It ain't like we got us a nice house and a lot of money like your family. But me and Mom are a family, too. We got each other."

I had always thought of our family as completely average, but I guess in Chigger's eyes we were pretty well off.

"You told your mom you had a lot of friends," I said. I knew I shouldn't have brought it up, but I felt obliged to say it.

Heat came into Chigger's eyes. "I'm just lookin' out for Mom, that's all. She's got enough on her mind without having to worry about me."

"I'm sorry," I said.

"Don't you go feeling sorry for me, or for Mom!" she snapped. "We can look out for ourselves!"

Before I could say another word she fled back down the path toward her house.

But I did feel sorry for Chigger, coming home to those empty rooms, not having a father around, and eating food out of cans. I knew it was wrong to feel that way. Once, I'd nursed an injured bird back to health, and the first thing it did was to fly away. Nobody, even the commonest sparrow, wanted pity. They might need some help, but only until they could be themselves again.

That afternoon Chigger didn't come back to my house, and I was brooding over her when, wouldn't you know it, Henry tore into the house shrieking, "I won! I won the contest!" I don't know what was more amazing—seeing him without a book or carrying the brand new Indianapolis model racecar.

"Who cares?" I said calmly, although I was sick with envy.

"Anybody can read," Will told him.

"Now I'm gonna get *my* picture in the newspaper," he said.

"So?" I snapped back.

"So you and Chigger are yesterday's news."

Although thoroughly depressed, out of principle I claimed, "Who wants a *plastic* car anyway?"

"Who wants chickens?" Henry countered.

Standing eyeball to eyeball, we glared at each other; then he chased me around the dining room table.

From the kitchen Mom shouted, "If my cake falls!"

Giving up the chase, Henry strode into the kitchen announcing, "Hey, Mom, I won that stupid contest!"

Wiping her hands on a dishtowel, Mom swelled with pride. "We'll have to have something special for dinner to celebrate, and for dessert we can go to the Tastee Freez for hot fudge sundaes!" Mom always looked forward to an opportunity to celebrate with lots of food, especially sweets, and I began to feel a little better about my brother's achievement.

"What would you like for dinner?" she asked Henry.

"How 'bout a couple of Luke and Chigger's chickens?" Will suggested.

"You're not touching any of our chickens!"

"Why not?" Henry sneered. "You only got a whole chicken ranch out there. You got to do something with them."

I stuck my nose in the air. "We're gonna keep them. They're pets."

"Who ever heard of having a hundred pet chickens?"

Actually, there were over two hundred now.

"And what are you going to do when school starts? Who's gonna feed those chickens then, and where are you going to keep them in cold weather?" he asked.

"In your bedroom."

"Why you...."

"If my cake falls!"

Henry halted immediately and in the brief calm that followed Will said, "I'll tell you what's gonna happen to those chickens. We're gonna eat 'em. One after another until they're all gone."

"You can't eat animals that you know personally," I contended.

"They're just stupid birds!" Henry countered.

"No, they're not. They...They...." I almost said that they had feelings, but it was really Chigger and I who had the feelings. "Just leave me alone!" I cried, tearing out of the house and slamming the door extra hard, although I'd been told a thousand times not to.

Even though Henry and I were brothers and supposed to hate each other, I really didn't mind his winning the Indy 500 racer, at least not too much. I generally fought out of principle. Any self-respecting brother would have done the same.

What bothered me was his calling after me, "It may not be us, but somebody's gonna eat those chickens!" He always had to have the last word, which really got to me, especially when he was right.

That week the *Daily Independent Gazette* published a bunch of letters to the editor prompted by the story about our chicken rescue operation, and conditions got better at the hatchery, at least to the extent that they didn't throw away any more chicks. I should have felt good about it, and I did, except that I'd hardly seen Chigger all week. And when I did see her, she acted kind of strange, sometimes very distant and the next instant like my best buddy. I thought it was because our having our picture in the paper hadn't been such a big deal, or at least not as big a deal as we'd hoped it would be.

Then, come Friday, we had to deal with our

poultry problem. Mom drew me aside and told me in a soft voice, "Your father found a farmer to give the chickens to."

"Aw, Mom."

"It's all part of growing up," she said.

"But how will I know they'll be all right?"

"They won't be treated any differently than any other chickens."

"But these chickens are special."

"You're just being a baby," Henry hissed at me.

I turned to Mom. "Maybe we shouldn't eat meat. I could be one of those...uh...."

"Vegetarians," Mom said.

"They're all beatniks and Communists," Henry informed us.

"How would you know?"

"I read about them this summer. At least I think I did."

Those vegetarians sounded creepy to me, but I persisted, "I can be one and still be an American, can't I?"

"I suppose," Mom said. "But remember we're Catholics, too."

Suddenly this was all becoming very confusing. "You mean Catholics can't be vegetarians?"

"Only on Fridays."

"Well, if we don't eat meat on Fridays, doesn't that make us part-time vegetarians?"

"We do it for religious reasons," Mom explained. "They only do it to be healthy."

I struggled to understand what she was talking about, but all these rules seemed made up by somebody, and not real at all. "Well," I said, "if we can be Catholics and Americans, why can't we be vegetarians, too?"

"Luke," Mom said with a sigh, "just do what you're told."

I knew that was the cue that Mom didn't want to hear any more about it, because she had run out of answers.

That evening when Dad got home we shaped clothes hangers into hooks and snagged each of the chickens by their scaly yellow legs. Then we stuffed the cackling birds into fruit crates we'd gotten behind Pearson's Grocery. By the time we got done the back of the station wagon was filled with the crates and several more were stacked and tied on the luggage rack on the roof.

We climbed into the car and headed down the street. I saw the curtain of Mrs. Filbert's window move as we passed by her house.

"Can we stop by Chigger's house?" I asked Dad as we rode along. I didn't want to stick my nose into her life, unless she wanted me to. But these were her chickens, too.

My friend was sitting on the doorstep when we pulled in the driveway next to her apartment with the car full of squawking birds. She seemed to grasp what we were doing, what we had to do, for which I was grateful, because I was so choked up that I couldn't speak.

Like a gentlemen, I got out and held the door for her. She slipped into the car without saying a word. Chigger and I simply rode along in the front seat with Dad, soberly looking ahead despite the riot of squawking and flapping going on all around us.

We drove out into the country, the farmhouses, barns, and silos swirling past us in the dusk.

"Days are already getting a little shorter," Dad

said.

Neither Chigger nor I responded.

We saw a series of Burma Shave signs, but that evening I didn't even bother to read any of the jingles.

The farm that Dad had located was rundown. Even the house wasn't painted. I mostly noticed the weeds and an old whetstone tilted in the doorway of the barn. I felt good that Dad had at least found a poor farmer who could use a ready-made flock of chickens.

A scrawny man in Oshkosh overalls emerged from the barn and hunkered over to the car. He hooted, "Them's some nice looking birds you got there."

With an air of pride, Chigger and I freed the chickens, which promptly ran through the weeds and under the house, which was set up on concrete blocks.

"Will they be warm enough this winter?" Chigger asked.

Glancing to Dad, the man chuckled, "They'll get plenty warm in my stew pot."

My ears burned.

"They can lay eggs, too!" Chigger sputtered at him.

"Not the roosters," he quipped.

I felt betrayed, yet I had known all along that this would be the fate of many of the chicks that I had lifted so tenderly out of the trash. I was standing among the adults now. Dad laid his hand on my shoulder. I knew he couldn't do anything for our chickens the way he had defended so many people in the war.

Someday Chigger and I will get married, I told myself as we drove home. We'll have our own egg farm and all the old hens would be retired as their just reward, and never have to be eaten. It struck me as a perfect future, except that I couldn't keep the tears from running down my face.

When we got back to my house I was thankful that Chigger stuck around for a while. In silence, we sat on the front porch swinging back and forth. "It ain't right," she said after a while.

"I know, after all we did for our chickens."

"It ain't right about *me* is what I mean," she explained. "I didn't care hardly enough about our chickens, 'least not as much as I did about myself. I was all the time thinking about becoming famous. I thought maybe people would, you know, like me, if I did something heroic. I thought being in the newspaper would solve all my problems."

"I like you," I told her. "And my mom and dad like you." I didn't mention my brothers and sister, because they didn't seem to like anybody. "We can go swimming tomorrow, or maybe to a movie. I promise not to be scared, at least not too much."

Chigger was shaking her head. "I been thinking and thinking on it, Luke, so much I thought my head was going to pop off. We just ain't the same kinds of people. I shouldn't have got you all mixed up with me. I seen that when you came over to my house. You got friends here and a lot of peace and quiet. All I've done is stir up a pot of trouble for you."

"What's the matter with you, Chig?" I asked.

"Nothin'. I just don't want to be hangin' around with you no more," she said, tears bursting into her eyes. Before I could stop her she jumped off the porch and tore off into the night.

XII.

THE NEXT DAY HENRY GOT HIS PICTURE in the newspaper, on the front page of the local section, clutching his model of a genuine Indianapolis 500 racecar. For the rest of the week there was no living with him. But as much as he bugged me, it was Chigger who had me so mixed up that I went around lightheaded 'most every day.

I guess the loss of our chickens, many of them heading toward a certain death, had hit both of us hard. But I couldn't see why she'd be mad at me. I wished we could go back to the carefree days we'd had earlier in the summer. Wasn't it our right as kids to enjoy each summer day without having to think about it so much?

I thought maybe I should talk to Dad about her, but he was always getting home late, and with the rest of the family around I never could find a good time for us to be alone.

Then, just a couple of weeks before Labor Day, the circus came to town, distracting me from the loss of the chickens and upstaging Henry's award and all other daily events, except Chigger, of course, who had become as much a part of my dreams and real-life fears as when I worried that my dad might have to go off at war again. I went downtown one morning to see the elephants on parade and to look for her. I suspected that nothing could keep Chigger away from a circus, and I was right. I found her surrounded by a bunch of kids from our class, including Buzz, Toby, and Gilman.

His yellowish-brown eyes flickering, Gilman was saying, "I 'spose now you're gonna tell us your dad was in the circus once."

Toby rolled his eyes heavenward. "Here we go again, and school ain't even started yet."

For once in her life Chigger was not bragging. In fact, she remained silent as a post.

"What was he?" Buzz asked her in a snotty tone of voice. "A lion tamer?"

Toby snorted, "Naw, he was a clown!"

Gilman grinned, "You sure he wasn't shot out of a cannon and landed on his head, like her?"

Ever so quietly, Chigger said, "Why don't you quit buggin' me for once? I just come here to see the elephants."

Of course, the guys took her call for a truce as an invitation to pick on her even more. "Guess we finally showed her," Buzz gloated. "Guess she's finally run out of stuff to lie about."

"Looks that way," said Gilman.

"Why don't you just leave her alone," I exclaimed.

"Why don't you run away and join the circus along with her?" Buzz said, whirling around to jut his jaw out at me.

"Can't you see you're hurting her feelings?" I asked hotly.

The three guys all chimed, "Awww!"

I stood there helplessly. How could I tell them to lay off her without telling them more about Chigger's tough family life, which would only give people more ammunition for gossip?

Buzz bragged, "Well, I'll tell you about my dad, and I ain't lying, like her. My dad's a doctor, and he took me up to his office the other day."

"So?" Chigger said, wrinkling her nose.

"So, he showed me an x-ray of a man that had drunk a Coke every day for over twenty years. His insides were all black and gooey."

Every x-ray I'd ever seen was black and I suspected that his dad was just trying to break Buzz's habit of drinking too much pop.

"It was probably an x-ray of your own potbelly," Chigger told Buzz, trying to act like she didn't care the least little bit.

Having guzzled plenty of soda pop, Toby asked nervously, "Black and gooey?

"Yeah," Buzz said. "And if it gets bad enough, it'll start to leak out your belly button!"

Patting his own jiggly stomach, Toby looked even more worried. But Chigger scoffed, "That ain't nothing but a bunch of bull."

"Well, he *is* a doctor," Buzz insisted. "He's important in this town and you ain't nothin' but a nobody. And that ain't no lie."

Luckily, we were interrupted by the elephants, which lumbered down Main Street, exotic in our small town. They paused in front of Mayor Ashcraft's house just long enough to unload an extraordinary amount of manure in his front yard. Needless to say they won our deepest admiration. Following the catcalls and squeals of laughter, the main topic of conversation that day had to do with the two questions: exactly how much manure the elephants had deposited on the mayor's doorstep, and who would be responsible for cleaning up the huge piles—the circus, the city, or the mayor himself? Most everybody agreed that the mayor should do it since he spread considerably more of the stuff himself, especially during election years.

Since it was a respectable newspaper, I knew the incident would never be mentioned in the *Daily Independent Gazette*, but we all knew that we had witnessed history in Roscoe, and that a detailed report of the event would be passed down through generations of old men on the liars' bench.

I used the opportunity the elephants gave us to say to Chigger, "Let's go get a cherry Coke."

I was positive Chigger would tell me where to go, right in front of the guys. But she sighed, "Well, all right. I sure got better things to do than listen to these dumbbells." As we headed to the Roscoe Cigar Store and Fountain she glanced back at Buzz. "I expect one Coke won't goo up my innards too much."

Cupping his hands around his mouth, Buzz called after her, "I think your brain's already gooed up!"

Chigger let that one go as we walked into the fountain and ordered our Cokes. As we twirled on the chrome stools, sipping the fizzy black pop, I didn't know what to say to her, especially since I couldn't get x-rays off my mind.

Finally, looking out the plate glass window, she said, "Them guys are a bunch of jerks."

I said, "Uh, you know, you don't have to let them bother you so much."

She blinked at me. "What the heck do you mean?"

"It doesn't really matter what people think or say, does it? Especially them."

"'Course not."

"So, don't pay any attention to them. Or even me, if I do something stupid."

"How can I not pay them any mind when they're teasing me all the time?"

"If you gave them a chance, maybe they'd get to like you, like I do."

"Are you kidding or what?" she cried out. Then, looking hard at me, she added, "I thought you was on my side."

"I am," I said. "I just want you to have some friends here, that's all. Maybe even a lot of friends, like you told your mom. School's starting soon and—"

"That's it, ain't it?" she said rearing up on the chrome stool. "When school starts you want to ditch me. You won't want to hang around with me no more."

"You're the one who won't hardly have anything to do with me lately," I pointed out. "Everybody already knows we're—what did Mom call that—an item, whatever that is. We had our picture in the newspaper together, holding hands and everything. It's just that you're my friend and I want you to be able to feel at home here. I want you to be happy." I tried to think of that quote from Abraham Lincoln, who they said had once slept in Roscoe, about how if you look for the good in people you'll always find it and if you look for the bad, you'll just as surely find it, too. Since I couldn't remember the quote exactly, I said, "Even Buzz isn't all bad. People just have to have a little pride."

She snorted. "What do you mean? Folks around here got everything. They got this whole town to themselves, just like you do, too. Only you don't realize how good you got it."

"Well, sort of, they do," I said. "And so do I.

But you scare them, because you've lived other places. They've spent all their lives here. They're maybe even jealous of you since you've lived in places they don't know anything about."

Chigger swelled. "Well, they ought to be. But that'd still be a first."

I knew what she meant, but found myself saying, "People here aren't much different from people anywhere else. They've got their good sides and their bad sides."

"All I've seen so far is their bad sides," she said.

"I'm sorry about that."

"What're *you* 'pologizing for? You ain't done nothin' but be my best friend in the whole wide world," Chigger said, glancing away from me. "But you can stop worrying about us. Truth is, I'm used to people treating me like Buzz and Toby and Gilman do. Besides, me and mom are gonna be movin' again soon. I probably won't even be around when that dumb ol' school starts again."

"Moving?" I asked, shocked. "Why?"

"Why not?" she said. "We ain't exactly hit it off here. Plus me and Mom got us a problem again."

I got the jitters as I asked, "What is it? Your dad?"

Eyes narrowed, she stared at me as if she was trying to see through me and back again. "This is a private, confidential secret," she said. "So I don't want you tellin' no one, not even your parents."

I wasn't in the habit of keeping secrets from my parents, especially Mom, who could pry just about anything out of me. But I told her, "I won't tell a soul. Now, what's happening? Is it your dad?"

"Yep."

"Maybe I can help you," I said, although I could

hardly catch my breath.

Chigger shook her head. "This one's a whopper, Luke. Bigger'n you and me put together."

"But you can't just leave," I told her. "You've got a home here. We've been friends all summer."

"My dad's on to where we're stayin'," she explained. "Mom got a letter from him just yesterday." Not even finishing her cherry Coke, which wasn't at all like Chigger, she slid off the chrome stool, "I'll let you know when me and Mom get ready to clear out of here. In the meantime, you don't wanna be hangin' out with me no more, Luke."

"I don't see why not," I protested.

She spun around and exclaimed, "You'll see when he gets here."

"But we're blood brother and sister," I reminded her.

"That's exactly why I don't want you hangin' around me," she said, this torn look in her eyes. "I don't want you gettin' hurt or nothin'. You're a big enough scaredy-cat as it is."

"Maybe my mom and dad could help," I said.

"Your mom and dad can't do nothin'!" Chigger cried out. "Nobody can do nothin' in this here world, Luke. Don't you know that? You just got to make out the best you can. That's what Mom says."

"I could at least talk to my parents about it."

"You promised not to tell 'em," Chigger said. "Besides, I'm sick of hearing about your parents! I'll tell you what you are! You're just jealous of me, like you said all the rest of them was!"

"What are you talking about?"

"'Cuz your dad is always workin' and you don't never get to see him! And he don't care nothin' about you nohow!"

Now that didn't make any kind of sense. I maybe didn't see enough of my dad, but he sure cared about us. What's more, I saw him more than Chigger saw her dad, which as far as I could tell was never, except when she didn't want to see him.

"Now you can just leave me alone!" she said. Before I could say anything she burst out the door and ran away, down toward the depot.

That day I wondered if Chigger wasn't the least little bit right about my dad, until he came home that evening with *eight* tickets to the circus. I ran as fast as I could over to her apartment. It seemed forever before she answered the door.

"We got tickets to the circus!" I exclaimed, thinking that would make it up to her.

"So? Didn't I just tell you that I didn't ever want to talk to you again?"

"My dad got one for you, too!"

She squinted at me. "Why? 'Cuz you all feel sorry for me?"

"No! Because we like you."

We peered at each other for a moment. Then she said, "All right, I'll go, but only 'cuz your dad done already bought that extra ticket."

I knew her mom was at work so I didn't know why I had this creepy feeling that somebody was in the apartment. The hair went up on the back of my neck, and I couldn't wait to get out of there. We ran full blast through the dark back to my house. I thought of asking Chigger about it, but figured she'd just tell me it was none of my beeswax.

I thought that every kid in America loved the circus. It was intrinsic to our species, Dad said, whatever that meant. That night my eyes were aglitter with the ringmaster, the clowns, the lady on the flying trapeze, the lion tamer, and the white horses circling the arena. But all evening Chigger seemed lost in her thoughts as she devoured an abundance of popcorn, peanuts, and cotton candy. She ate even more food than usual, prompting Mom to whisper to Dad, "That Chigger's a sideshow in and of herself."

She didn't say it meanly, but I was still glad Dad answered, "She's a growing girl, that's all."

"As much as she eats and she's still as skinny as a spider," Mom said.

Dad ordered more hot dogs.

I knew Chigger had a monstrous appetite, and I knew Mom would love to fatten her up, but I had never seen her eat so much. It was like she had to fill up a big, sad hole inside herself. Sitting next to her, I asked, "Isn't this great, being here at the circus and getting to eat all this stuff?"

"Oh, sure," Chigger said dreamily, absorbed in chewing another handful of peanuts.

She hardly said a word to me that evening, so when we got home, I said, "Why don't we sit on the front porch a while and talk. You know, about the circus and stuff."

"I better get on home," she said, deadpan.

"You don't have to stay long," I suggested.

"Didn't you hear me? I said I gotta get home!"

"Come on, just stick around for a little while," I urged.

"I can't. It's late!"

I knew that wasn't it. Left to her own devices, Chigger would have stayed out all night, every night. Licking my lips and wiping my hands on my jeans, I asked, "Mind if I walk home with you?"

"No! I mean, yes, I do mind! Knowin' you, you'd be afraid to walk back in the dark all by yourself. Besides, I don't want you comin' nowhere near my house no more! You hear me? Just leave me alone. I don't need you, or nobody! How many times have I got to tell you? I don't like you no more, Luke. I don't like you or nobody! And I don't want no one likin' me!" Tearing across the yard, she vanished into the dark.

Now I was positive that something ominous was happening at her home. I could feel it in my bones. Chigger might be looking out for me, but it still didn't make sense for her to abandon me right when she had such a big problem. It seemed to me that she needed a friend now more than ever in her life.

No sooner was she gone than Henry appeared in the doorway, nodding like an expert. He said, "You know, girls are like that."

Staring off into the dark after Chigger, I grumbled, "How would you know?"

Rocking back and forth on his heels, Henry grinned at me as if he knew something I didn't.

I sneered, "Is that something you read about this summer?"

"Nope," he said in the most self-satisfied manner. "I learned it through direct, firsthand experience."

Suspiciously, I squinted at him.

"You know Carol Latham?" he asked.

I almost said, "You mean that snotty, stuck-up girl in your class," but contented myself with making a face, like I was getting sick to my stomach.

Henry boasted, "I French kissed her once, behind the concession stand at the park. You know the place."

I thought of making some remark about his fish

face being good for puckering up, but just said, "So?" I tried to act unimpressed, especially since I didn't know the difference between French kissing and French fries. Besides, I figured Henry was lying anyway.

Looking haughty, like he was an old pro at this romantic stuff, Henry explained, "When a girl acts like she doesn't like you, that means she really does like you—a lot!"

I stopped cold. I didn't know why, but somehow that made sense to me.

XIII.

THE NEXT MORNING I WENT to Harold's Barbershop for my regular scalping. Every other week we got haircuts whether we needed them or not. As usual, Dad got me there first thing, before the crowd. My one consolation was that with autumn coming on I was allowed to let my GI haircut grow out again, until my hair was all of an inch and a half long on top.

I liked the barbershop, where I could be around the men and listen to their stories and corny jokes, especially since Chigger had dropped out of my life. I kept trying to convince myself that men had more sense. They didn't just up and abandon their friends. I decided that from now on I should hang out with my own kind. No matter what people said about growing up, I wasn't about to have anything in the world to do with girls, not ever again.

The fragrance of Wildroot hair tonic hung around me as I sat in the chair. It was so early that besides Harold and me, the only other people in the barbershop were a woman with her son and baby.

I was uncomfortable because Henry, Will, and Greg weren't there. It didn't feel right getting a Saturday morning haircut without having to fight over who was going to be first. But it was mostly Chigger who had me out of sorts. Then the baby started to cry.

Harold seemed especially jumpy, not at all like he was when the usual group of men were around. He sighed over the noise. "Real hot spell we've been having, huh?"

"Yes sir," I said, sitting up rigidly in the chair, extremely conscious of my ears, because Harold was known to let his clippers stray. Then right there in public the woman started to nurse her baby.

Harold stopped in mid-sentence, like his whole body had locked up on him. "Ahem…." He waved the clippers randomly, in the vicinity of my head. I thought he was going to tell the lady, "You wanna go outside and do that. This is a public business, you know." Instead, his hand wobbling more than ever, his voice rising an octave, he muttered to me, "Sure has been hot. I'm about ready for autumn myself."

I gulped. "Yes sir."

I snatched glimpses of the woman out of the corner of my eye. Harold had turned the chair away from her, just enough so it wouldn't be obvious that he was trying to avoid looking at her, and keep me from doing the same. His voice continuing to rise, he said, "Yes sir, I can't wait for, ahem, squirrel season, ahem, it'll be starting, ahem, in just a few weeks."

The woman seemed less jittery than us, especially Harold. Not bothering with anyone, the baby suckled quietly. When Harold had finished scalping me, he doused my head with hair tonic, unhooked the apron, which as usual had been strangling me, gave it a snap as he lifted it off me, then brushed me off with a little whisk broom. I got out of the chair and gave him seventy-five cents, the going rate for a haircut in Roscoe, then treated myself to a good scratching session—

neck, shoulders, stomach, and as much of my back as I could reach. Harold never seemed to take offense at this reaction to his haircuts; at least if he did he didn't show it. Then while I waited for Dad to pick me up, I sat spinning in the extra chair, snatching glimpses of the woman with each turn. She looked as sweet as the Virgin Mary as she nursed the child—calm, quiet, and at peace with herself—so I didn't know why she made me think of Chigger.

The woman's son, who must have been starting first grade, sat through his haircut and came out of it with only a few nicks to the head. Harold shook hair tonic onto the boy's head, working it into the scalp with his fingers, then neatly combed his hair across the crown of his head, with a little bump in the front—just like mine and every other boy in America in 1959.

He freed the kid from the chair and told the woman, who had meanwhile re-buttoned her blouse, "That'll, ahem, be seventy-five cents."

As she paid Harold she looked admiringly upon her son, her hand resting on his shoulder as they left the barbershop. Harold didn't seem to relax until a group of men clumped into the shop, Dad among them. They held the door for the woman, but otherwise ignored her as they talked of hunting. One of them asked Harold, "You still got that squirrel gun you been trying to sell?"

"Maybe."

The man laughed, glancing to the other guys for support. "What do you mean 'maybe'? You either got it or you don't."

"A fellow's been looking to buy it. New around here," Harold explained; then he turned to Dad and asked, "Unless you're interested in the rifle, Major?" He nodded toward me. "For the boy."

Around town they called my father "Major," which always made me smile inside, knowing he was respected and we had a place within the community.

Dad looked to me.

Lost in a mood, I was staring out the window at the railroad station. Flanked by glistening brick streets, the depot had broad eaves, under which stood iron-wheeled baggage carts. Dad smiled at me. "Oh, I don't know if Luke's got much heart for guns." He often accused me of being a dreamer, and in the next breath told me I was much like him when he was a boy.

"Sure that gun shoots straight?" one of the men kidded Harold as he passed through the curtained doorway to get the rifle from the back room.

"I guarantee it!" he called over his shoulder.

I was still drawn to the window when Harold handed me the gun, saying, "Here, boy, try this out for size." The stock felt smooth against the palms of my hands. Harold claimed it had just been cleaned, and it did smell richly of gun oil. I tucked the butt into my left shoulder.

"Lefty, huh?" a man remarked.

Hands in his pockets, Dad rocked back and forth on his heels, not saying a word. The bolt cool in my hand, I cocked the gun, careful to point it away from people.

"It's just a bolt-action .22," someone said, "but it ought to be good enough for squirrels and tin cans."

As far as I was concerned, I was Davy Crockett stalking the wilds for grizzly bears and cougars. They gave me some basic lessons, which I already knew, such as keep the safety on, point the barrel to the ground, and never assume it's unloaded.

"Do you want it?" asked Dad.

For the life of me I couldn't think what I would use it for. I wasn't about to shoot any animals. But with Chigger acting so strange and having lost my other friends, I had become thoroughly confounded of late. I thought I might become a sober man among men if I had a gun. I might become a hero like my father.

"Sure," I said, grinning ear to ear.

Dad looked away from me, like that hadn't been the answer he'd expected from me. I almost said, "I changed my mind," when a stranger stomped into the barbershop. Thinly built, with black hair like crow feathers, he had a handsome, square-jawed face except that he needed a shave. He wore dirty blue jeans with the knees torn out, and a white t-shirt with a package of cigarettes rolled into the sleeve.

With a limp that put a wince on his face with each step, he walked over to us. Not even nodding hello to anyone, he asked Harold, "That the gun?"

"Yep," Harold said.

Looking over the rifle in my hands, the man said, "I'll give you fifteen bucks for it. Not a penny more."

"I done already sold it," Harold said.

Frowning bitterly, the man snarled, "Looks like a piece of junk anyway. Probably blow up in my face." Without another word he turned and limped toward the door. I could tell everybody was nervous, not only because this man was new around here, but also because he was so unfriendly. As the stranger opened the door one of the men called after him, "You lookin' to do some squirrel huntin'?"

"Maybe," he said, his lip curling, and hobbled out into the brightening day.

"I'll pick the gun up later," Dad said. "I don't want

to go walking around town with a gun in my hands."

That broke the tension about the stranger.

"'Specially not into the bank!" someone joked.

While Dad went to the hardware store, he gave me a dime to get a Coke at the Roscoe Cigar Store and Fountain. "Just consider it a bonus for hazardous duty," he said. We smiled at each other, because he often likened going to Harold to being in combat. When I strolled into the drugstore, Buzz, Toby, and Gilman were seated at the marble counter.

"Looks like you got scalped," Buzz said, spinning on a chrome stool.

Gilman shaped his lips into an *O* and beat them Indian style.

I slid onto a stool, not minding their kidding me. It had a different tone from when they were picking on Chigger, and I was glad to be hanging out with them again.

Punching me on the arm, Gilman asked, "Where's your girlfriend?"

Suddenly I felt a deep emptiness running right down to my feet. "Oh, she's around somewhere, I guess."

"You were smart to ditch her," Toby said.

"Well…." I couldn't say anything when actually she had abandoned me.

"She's about as popular around here as a skunk," Buzz said.

Clifford, the soda jerk, asked, "What'll ya have, bud?"

"Cherry Coke." I just loved the taste of the sweet syrup in the fizz of the cola. Then again I also loved chocolate. "Wait a minute, how about a chocolate Coke?"

Clifford gave me his what-a-stupid-kid look. "Make up your mind."

"Maybe…."

Clifford dribbled his fingers on the marble counter. "Come on, kid. I ain't got all day!" I glanced around. There wasn't another customer within a block of the Cigar Store and Fountain.

"Give him some of both," Buzz suggested.

I perked up. "You can do that?"

"Natch."

My three old friends raised their pear-shaped glasses. Buzz said, "What do you think we're having?"

With those practical jokers I knew I was taking my chances, but I tried the combination and liked the curious blend of flavors. Suddenly it was great to be back with my friends in our safe little town. Knowing I really had one up on them, I declared, "I've got a gun!"

Clifford stopped cold, right beside the cash register, and started to raise his hands.

The four of us nearly fell off our stools we were laughing so hard.

"Reach for the sky!" Buzz kidded.

"Very funny." Clifford scowled as he went back to wiping the counter. "You know, I ought to kick your little butts outta here."

"Then you wouldn't have any customers at all," Gilman said.

Buzz sniggered, "Now I know why they call 'em soda jerks."

Clifford decided to check on the stock in the back room and the guys eagerly turned back to me. "You mean you got a *real* gun?" asked Buzz.

"My dad just bought it from Harold. We're going to pick it up later." I chuckled. "We didn't want to go walking around town with a gun, especially into the bank."

Toby's mouth hung open. "That's for sure. That was smart of you."

I punched him on the arm. "It was a joke. Don't you get it?"

He stared blankly at me.

I didn't bother trying to explain it to him and for the next few minutes the questions about the gun flew at me.

"What kind of gun is it?"

"Twenty-two."

"Automatic?"

"Bolt action."

Toby concluded the conversation by saying, "Aw, that ain't nothing. My brother Albert's got a twenty-gauge shotgun."

Still I knew that he and the other guys were in awe. I told them about the weird guy who'd stomped into the barbershop to look at the gun.

"He probably just wanted to shoot tin cans," Buzz said. "Or maybe rats out at the town dump."

Although he was pretty mean looking, I convinced myself, "Yeah, I'm sure he wasn't planning to shoot anyone."

"My dad says there are a lot of bums passing through town these days," Toby said. "He says it's getting almost as bad as in the Depression."

Gilman added, "Fred the Junkman's the only tramp we like to have around here."

Changing the subject, Buzz suggested, "Let's go see what's showing at the Palace this afternoon."

"Uh, okay," I said, telling myself that I could make myself sit through a horror movie, and even if

I couldn't, it would be worth it to be back with the guys. We downed the rest of our Cokes, headed out the door, and ran smack into Chigger out on the sidewalk. Standing among my old friends, I felt like a traitor, yet she had told me to leave her alone, and why shouldn't I have fun with my other friends, too? What I really wanted was for everybody to be friends, even if they didn't like each other.

Not quite looking at her, I said, "Hi, Chig."

She got a tight look around her eyes as she stared back at me.

Buzz punched me on the arm and said, "Come on, Luke, let's split."

"Yeah," Toby said. "Something smells bad around here. Real bad."

I stood there frozen, prompting Chigger to ask me, "What're you gawking at?"

As she turned away from us, Gilman suggested, "Let her go, Luke. She's nothing but trouble, 'specially now that her dad's in town."

"Her dad's in town?" I asked. "For certain?"

"Yeah, and you ought to see him!" Buzz laughed.

Toby burst out, "He sure ain't any gee-whizz-o-gist, or whatever that was! He's a bum with a capital B."

The three of them had to sit down on the curb to get their laughter under control. Immediately, I thought of the stranger at the barbershop. Before I could say another word, Chigger glanced back at us and sprinted down the street, as though she couldn't wait to get as far away from them—and me—as possible.

Thereafter, the rumors of Chigger's dad flew around Roscoe. People said he'd been in the army, prison, a nuthouse, and, more likely, California.

He was, in fact, the man who had stopped by the barbershop. If he ever got himself cleaned up, he could have been as handsome as those guys on the soap operas that Mom claimed she didn't watch. But he was always a couple of days behind in shaving and his t-shirts were the color of an overcast sky. Like Chigger's mom, he looked too young to be a parent, at least of a twelve year old. What was most amazing about him was that he began to appear on Main Street "under the influence," as Mom called it, not every night, but enough to make people edgy.

Fulton County, for which Roscoe was the county seat, had always been dry. In fact, people often kidded that Prohibition had gotten its start in our town. Mom in particular, who indulged in nothing more than a glass of Mogen David wine once a year at Christmas time, was beside herself. One morning she said, "You stay away from…" I thought she was going to say Russell Heck. "…from Chigger."

"Why?"

"Is it because her dad's from California?" Sis asked. "Huh, Mom?"

Mom frowned. "Not really. Well, partly."

"Everybody's crazy out there, aren't they, Mom?" Henry said in a know-it-all tone.

"Well…." Mom had to think that over. "Maybe not everybody."

"But that's where they invented hula hoops," Will protested.

Trying to steer the discussion back to the real issue, I said, "I can see why I should stay away from her father, but why Chigger?"

"Just because."

"He doesn't live with them," I argued. "He was staying there for a day or two, but I heard he's got a room at the Burton Tourist Home now."

"I just don't want you associating with their family at all," Mom said firmly.

Although I had seen neither hide nor hair of Chigger for days, I persisted, "But *why*? You always liked Chigger."

"I still do," Mom said, softening around the eyes. "But there's something going on there that I don't want you to get mixed up in."

"Like what?"

"It's a domestic situation."

"A what?"

"You'll understand when you're older."

Tired of that standard answer, I went outside for some fresh air.

"Don't you go over there," Mom called after me, her jaw working hard as she ground her teeth. "I don't want you to get hurt!"

If I could get hurt, then so could Chigger, and her mom. And her dad had been trying to buy a gun. He hadn't gotten it, but they were as easy to obtain as tools in a hardware store. What scared me most were my worries about *why* he wanted a gun.

Despite Mom's advice about staying away from Chigger, the next day I ran into her downtown. Stepping right in front of her so she couldn't get away too easily, I asked, "Hey, you wanna come over to my house tonight? We can sit out on the porch. We don't have to do anything. We can just sit there. You don't even have to talk to me if you don't want to."

She shook her head. "My mom said I shouldn't."

Before I could say anything else she turned back

down the street, leaving me more worried than ever. She seemed so small when she was quiet.

Two days later, the guys and I went downtown to the Saturday matinee, and the four of us found ourselves standing in line directly behind Russell Heck. Smoking continually, he ground out one butt after another on the sidewalk, right in public, and kept complaining: "What the hell's holding up this line?"

I recognized the smell of whiskey on a person's breath from times when I'd visited the officers' club on the Air Force base, and also from trips to Indianapolis and Louisville, which were so full of people "under the influence" that whenever we went there Mom spent the whole day telling us, "Don't touch *anything.*" It was easy not to touch anything in those cities, where the extent of our corruption was eating stacks of those small White Castle hamburgers. However, it was difficult to avoid Russell Heck, standing in a line of kids pushing forward to get into a horror movie. I stared at him every chance I could get, trying to decide whether he could be violent or not.

Buzz kept elbowing me and whispering, "So glad I am, so sad I'll be, if I can't find the bathroom key."

"What's that supposed to mean?" I asked.

"Drunks always have to go pee," he said. "A lot."

Gilman tilted his arm toward his face to make like he was guzzling whiskey.

Every time Russell Heck turned around, the guys instantly put on angel faces. Then Buzz began to shove Toby ahead in the line so he kept bumping into Russell Heck. The man finally whirled around and yelled, "You wanna get your belly out of my behind, fat boy!"

"S...s...sorry." Toby just about strangled before he could get the word out, after which, at the risk of people cutting in on us, we remained a good three feet behind Russell Heck.

The horror movie was nothing compared to being around Russell Heck. He literally made the hair stand up on the back of my neck, even after my haircut, and I wondered how Chigger could stand having him for a father. He seemed both pitiful and menacing, like a stray dog that would bite you if you got too close, even if you were just trying to give him some food. When we went into the theater, Buzz wanted to sit behind him, but I said, "That's pushing our luck." In the end, we sat as far away from the man as possible.

After that, we often saw Russell Heck at the theater, whenever there was a horror or action film, which mostly attracted kids. We heard that he also spent a good portion of his time at the Wrong Number Tavern, over in Oglesby.

"What's he doing here?" was the question people most often asked. The answer that made the most sense was that he was mooching off his ex-wife, Chigger's mom. "She sort of has to bribe him," Buzz said. "My mom says he leaves them alone as long as she gives him money for rent and booze. He don't bother to eat."

Gilman added, "My mom says they probably got married when they were just teenagers, and they had Chigger by mistake."

I figured Buzz would make a joke about Chigger being a mistake, but for once in his life he kept his mouth shut.

One day I overheard Mom talking on the phone to Mrs. Filbert, and for once it wasn't about chickens. She was saying, "No, he doesn't work. Doesn't have to. He's got some sort of disability pension coming from the military. He does have that limp, but I bet there's something wrong with his head, too." Being a deadbeat was just about the worst thing a person could be in Roscoe, and he was apparently that, as well as a drunk, and a whole lot more. It was the whole lot more that bothered me, because you could see the lack of light in his eyes. "Yes, I agree," Mom spoke into the phone. "People like that are a disgrace, plain and simple."

Then Buzz claimed, "He's some kind of war hero. He seen something terrible in Korea that won't leave his mind. That's what my dad says."

We were downtown sitting on the liars' bench, swinging our legs back and forth, and suddenly I was sweating all over, thinking about my father flying combat missions, thinking what would have happened if he had never come home. When Chigger walked by, Buzz, who was actually trying to be friendly for once in his life, said to her, "I hear your dad got injured bad in the war."

She snarled at him, "Drop dead."

That made Russell Heck even more of a mystery.

I had to admit that he was the first man I'd ever seen up close who had a real tattoo—a screaming eagle on his right forearm.

For a while people were ready to give Russell Heck the benefit of the doubt, until Sheriff Browner, worried that a criminal element had infiltrated Roscoe, requested information about him from the Army. He learned that he was no hero. He had served his two years and been honorably discharged, though he had seen action in Korea.

Only Dad said anything in Russell Heck's favor, "He was an infantryman. Those guys had it tough in Korea. They got ground up on the front and then sent right home, without any help readjusting to civilian life." Dad added, "Some of those men are still fighting the war."

Then, just a week or so before the start of school, Russell Heck was arrested on the square. He had been sleeping on the park bench at the foot of the copper statue of a World War I doughboy. The next day the newspaper headline in the local section read "Man Arrested for Vagrancy." Although he was released after paying a small fine, he was more than ever the topic of conversation around town. When I caught up with the guys downtown Buzz was saying, "My dad says we need a town drunk. We haven't had one for years."

Although Chigger hadn't said one word about her father to anyone since he'd shown up in town, the guys kept reminding me that he'd fallen a little bit short of her previous claims.

"She ought to be on that show, *Truth Or Consequences*," said Toby.

"Yeah, and *To Tell the Truth*," Gilman added.

Buzz told me, "Her dad's already made more news than you and Chigger put together."

XIV.

WORRIED ABOUT CHIGGER MOST EVERY MINUTE, I finally got up enough nerve to go over to her house. It was just days before the start of school and I was worried that she wouldn't be with us in sixth grade. No one was there, or at least nobody answered the door. The place actually looked unoccupied. I returned home with a queasy feeling.

"Where have you been?" asked Mom the moment I walked in the door.

I looked down at my feet. "I went to see if Chigger was still around."

I thought I was going to catch it for disobeying her, but she only asked, "Haven't you heard?"

My heart was in my throat. "Did she move away?"

Mom shook her head. "Not yet, but she may have to."

"Have to?" I asked.

Mom stirred intently with a wooden spoon in a large mixing bowl cradled in her left arm. "There's been a lot of stealing going on lately."

"So? What's that got to do with Chigger?"

I'd heard about somebody breaking into the poor box at the Methodist Church, but that hadn't exactly been big news. Mrs. Filbert had even complained that the Methodists deserved it, since they were always such bleeding hearts. She said they should know better than to just leave their money lying around like that.

Mom said, "Somebody broke into the pop machine in front of the grocery last night."

My mouth dropping open, I asked, "Don't they have any idea who's doing it?"

Mom frowned. "Around town people are saying that Russell Heck's a drunk and it won't be long before he becomes a jailbird, too—for theft."

"Aw, Mom," I said, although I wouldn't have put it past him. I just felt so sorry for Chigger. I hated all this gossip, which depended so much on exaggerating and mixing up the truth to make it more exciting and to assure the conclusion people already had in mind. "What makes them think it's Russell Heck?"

"When they're desperate for money, people will do just about anything, Luke," Mom said. "We never had any crime in town until he showed up, and now we've got a whole crime wave."

"I'm sure it's not him," I said, not for his sake, but for Chigger's.

"We'll see."

"What do you mean?"

She kept cranking the wooden spoon in the bowl, making another cake from scratch. "I'll tell you, on one condition. You're not to breathe a word of this to *anyone*. Promise?"

I gulped and mumbled, "Sure."

She shook a finger at me. "If word gets out the whole thing will be ruined." She actually looked over her shoulder to see if any of my brothers or Sis were around to hear, then she leaned in my direction and spoke secretively. "They're laying a trap for him. They figure he'll hit the coin box on the newsstand in front of the *Daily Independent Gazette* next. If and when he does, they'll get him. Sheriff Browner has it staked out."

"Oh." I was shocked, but also thought to ask, "Uh, when?"

"Tonight."

That evening while Will and Sis were having a pillow fight in one of the bedrooms upstairs and Henry was polishing his racecar for the five hundredth time, Mom asked Dad, "Are you going out there tonight?"

They were sitting on the porch. Dad shook open the newspaper and said, "No, I'm not."

"Why not?"

"I've got better things to do than chase after some petty thief."

"Sheriff Browner might need help."

Dad snorted. "I'll leave that to the people who enjoy that sort of thing. I expect he'll have plenty of volunteers. As much as they're against crime, a lot of people seem to be just plain thrilled by it."

"Well, I hope they nab him soon. There's hardly a place left in town to rob, except the gumball machine at Woolworth's and it's inside those thick glass doors."

They had a perfect right to catch a thief, I thought, although I didn't want Chigger to get hurt any more than she already had been. In fact, I hoped her dad would be arrested and sent away to jail for a good, long time. That way Chigger and her mom could stay in town without being any more humiliated than they already had been. They might begin to feel safe and, in time, people might even come to like them.

Later that night, when everybody else was asleep, I lay awake staring at the cracks in the ceiling. Finally,

I got up and, quiet as can be, climbed out my bedroom window onto the front porch roof and down the lattice of honeysuckle.

I could barely see my own feet as I picked my way along the path across the pasture to her home. Above me the black leaves were a-swirl with wind. I was so scared being outside alone in the dark that I could hardly catch my breath.

There were lights on in Chigger's apartment, seeping out along the edges of the blinds, and quarreling voices. I couldn't make out what they were saying, but most of the noise was coming from Russell Heck.

Chills running up and down my spine, I crept forward out of the dark to the small porch, which led up the stairs.

"Luke?"

I froze.

"Chigger?"

"Who else?" We stood in the dark for a while, hardly able to see one another, just listening to each other's breathing. Then she asked, "What the heck are you doin' here?"

I wanted to ask her why she was standing there in the dark at the bottom of the stairs, but I just said, "I, uh, I was worried about you."

"Ain't nothin' about me to bother yourself over."

"But I haven't seen you for so long."

"I told you I been busy."

"What's going on? Can't you tell me?"

"We don't belong here, that's all."

"What about this summer? I thought you liked being with me, with my family. What about our chickens and everything?"

"Our chickens are gone, remember? That weren't nothin' but wishful thinking. They was all just kilt and eaten."

"Not all of them. Some of the chickens are living and breathing right this very minute. And besides, it meant a whole lot to me, you know, being with you. Even though we're old news now we still got our picture in the paper and all. It happened. We did something good. We really did. Nobody can take that away from us."

Stepping forward into the soft light of the moon, she looked at me a while, the edges of her eyes turning silver in the light, and I was sure she'd start crying any second. She said quietly, "You and your family's been real good to me, Luke, but you know the others, how they've treated me. Boy, I wanted to be famous so bad, like when we got our picture in the paper. But now I'm too famous. Everybody knows too much about Mom and me, and I can't hardly walk down the street without people laughing at me. Right now I'd give anything to be a nobody again."

"People don't laugh at you," I protested.

"Like heck they don't. What about Buzz, Toby, and Gilman?"

"They aren't people. They're just kids, like us."

"Well, I know everybody's gossiping about us. It's humiliating."

I couldn't think of a soothing word to say to her.

She shook her head. "Me and Mom got to go somewheres again where nobody knows us."

I glanced upstairs, toward the quarreling voices.

"They're talkin' it over, but no matter what, we're clearing out of here first chance we get. It ain't safe for us here no more, not with what he's been threatening to do to us."

"Do what?" I asked breathlessly.

"I ain't sayin'."

"Do what?" I insisted.

She looked away from me like she was ashamed. "Like I done told you already, he's pretty good with his fists, 'specially when he don't get his way. And he blames Mom for everything that's ever gone wrong in his life."

I was sick to my stomach. Chigger was right. He was worse than the movies. Still I insisted, "You can't leave!"

She snorted. "Whaddaya mean we can't? We done it plenty of times before and we'll sure as heck have to do it again, if we wanna keep on living."

"But…but…I don't want you to go, Chigger."

She looked at me really funny with that soft light she'd had in her eyes when she'd first come into our class. "Well, I can't do nothin' about that now, can I?"

"Maybe I can help you."

"You can't do nothin'! You're just a kid like me and we can't do nothin'. There ought to be a law in the Constitution sayin' we got rights, too. But there ain't, so there. We ain't got rights to do nothin' except what we're told. Believe me, if somethin' could've been done, I'd've done it myself a long time ago. Now you just stay away from here. This here is a personal private family matter!"

"He'll hunt you down again, won't he?" I asked Chigger. "And then what?"

"Leastways Mom and me got a chance," she said. "We're always hopin' he won't find us. Don't you see? If we don't get shed of him, he's gonna do something bad to Mom. I just know it. And probably to me, too."

"Running won't work, Chigger," I said, my throat so dry I could hardly get the words out.

She snorted. "How do you know?"

I shrugged. "I don't know, not for sure. But my dad says you can never run away from anything, and that makes sense to me. He says—"

"What else can we do?" she cut in. "He's all crazy and mixed up. It's like he hates us, but can't live without us either."

"Why don't you call the police?" I asked. "Sheriff Browner could help."

"Police can't do nothin', at least not until someone is already hurt bad or kilt dead. Now I don't wanna talk about it no more! We don't have no other choice, Luke! That's all there is to it!" she cried and ran up the stairs. Just as she got to the landing at the top the door exploded open, barely missing her, and Russell Heck staggered down the steps.

"What the hell?" he yelled when he banged into me, standing at the bottom of the stairs. Shoving me aside, he disappeared into the night shouting over his shoulder, "I'll be back, Gloria! You can't treat me that way! Not anymore! This is the last straw! And don't you try and run off on me again. You do that, and it's over with you. I'll be watching, you hear?"

I was left standing face to face with Chigger, down the length of stairs.

"What's the matter?" Chigger asked. "I thought I told you to scat."

"I can't."

Clenching her teeth and closing her fists, she stomped back down the stairs. "I said to get outta here!"

I was sure she was going to try to knock my

block off, but I just stood there, telling her, "I can't. There's something important I've got to tell you."

"What?" she asked.

"Uh, they're trying to catch your dad tonight."

"Catch my dad? What for?"

I had promised Mom, but Chigger was a true blue friend and besides, if Mom knew about the stakeout, everybody else in town must also have heard about it. So I told Chigger about the thefts. "Maybe if he promises to get help," I said. "Dad says they have places, like veterans hospitals, to help people like him. We can tell him not to break into the coin box on the newsstand. Then he'll go away and get some help. Then you can stay here and everything will be all right."

Chigger seemed totally perplexed. "What are you talking about?"

"Down at the newspaper office," I said. "They got people waiting to nab him if he tries to break into the coin box."

Her upper lip curled. "What do you mean?"

"In Roscoe there's never any crime. Once somebody's bicycle got stolen—or they thought it was. But it turned out that the guy's brother had just borrowed it. That's the closest we've come to a real crime since I've lived here. Now, like my mom says, we got a crime wave on our hands."

Chigger's face turned red. "Since my dad's a drunk and a bum, you think he's a crook, too?"

"I didn't mean to accuse him. I…I'm sorry. I didn't mean to jump to conclusions. I—"

"You don't need to apologize, 'cuz for all I know he may be a thief too, all right!" Chigger snapped.

"What should we do?"

"I don't know."

Although unsure what to do, without saying another word to each other, we headed downtown to the Burton Tourist Home. We hid in the shadows across the way, at the mouth of the alley.

"Are you sure we're doing the right thing?" Chigger asked.

"No," I said immediately. "I'm not even sure what we're doing."

I couldn't decide whether to warn him or not, or even how to do so. It seemed to me that he was a bully and a whiner, all wrapped up in one. Neither of us, especially Chigger, wanted to face him. Then I thought of leaving a note, warning him to get help or else.

"I could write it," I said. "He doesn't know my handwriting."

Chigger snorted, "You think he knows mine?"

"I could write, 'Police are after you. Better mend your ways.'" I wanted to add, "And leave town *immediately*." But I didn't have a pencil or a piece of paper and anyway Chigger sighed, "It won't work. You don't know my dad. He ain't got any sense anymore. He needs one of them headshrinkers, but he'd never admit it. He says we're all crazy and trying to get him. Besides, it ain't right to tip him off, neither." She hung her head. "Fact is, I'd just as soon see him arrested. 'Least that way he wouldn't be able to get at Mom and me for a while."

We ended up watching the light in his window, figuring that way we'd know where he was. I was mainly concerned with protecting Chigger and felt that, here in the night, she was safe, if only because we were together.

Within minutes, leaning against each other, our heads knocking together like a couple of coconuts, we had both fallen asleep. When we awoke it seemed very late, at least it was very dark and still. The light was off in the room.

Tired, aching from being scrunched against the cold brick wall, I wanted to go home, but Chigger said, "Let's go downtown and see if they caught, you know, if…."

"All right," I mumbled, not quite looking at her.

Whether she wanted me to or not, I slipped my hand in hers as we walked along. I swore to myself that no matter what happened I would always stand by her, even if Buzz and the guys never spoke to me again.

Except for Monday night shopping, an occasional Friday movie with my parents, and the night we'd had our picture taken for the newspaper, I had never been downtown after five p.m. As we stumbled along, it occurred to me that we should be careful not to get caught ourselves.

Downtown was deathly quiet. The color had been leached out of the storefronts, which normally competed among themselves with the loudest and most ugly advertisements.

"There's nobody here," murmured Chigger.

This creepy feeling running all through my body, I whispered, "I wouldn't be so sure."

No sooner were the words out of my mouth than a silhouetted figure crept down the sidewalk on the other side of the street. The misty yellow light of the streetlamps cast long shadows of him, which folded in half up the sides of the buildings and blinked at each doorway opening. Arriving at the newspaper office, he took a crowbar from inside his shirt and began to pry at the lock on the newsstand. There was a clinking sound of metal, which echoed up and down the empty street. The man glanced left and right, then went back to prying open the lock. Presently the lock snapped and the culprit grabbed at the coins in the box. Almost simultaneously a bank of car headlights turned on and we heard Sheriff Browner's booming voice: "Hold it right there, you skunk!"

The thief turned to run, but Sheriff Browner warned, "We'll shoot!"

Moments later, the suspect was handcuffed and out of every nook and cranny came about a hundred of our friends and neighbors. Mom had warned me to keep it a secret. However, from the looks of it, not only did everybody in town know about the stakeout, but most everybody had also been deputized.

Chigger and I squeezed through the crowd.

"I'm just about tore apart!" Chigger said, hanging on to me for dear life. "I want it to be him. But if it's him, I won't hardly be able to stand it!"

It cut into me like a knife, too—to wish that my best friend's father would be caught in the act, that he should be arrested and put into jail.

We strained for a closer look.

Finally someone shouted, "It's Albert Lee!"

"Who?" Chigger asked.

My mouth dropped open. "Toby's big brother."

We reached the front of the crowd and stuck our heads into the opening, which the sheriff had cleared, and got a good look at him. Plump-faced with small, piggish eyes, just like Toby, he blinked back into the lights aimed upon him from all directions.

XV.

THE NEXT MORNING MOM RAGED, "I was worried sick about you, Luke!"

"Nothing happened," I mumbled.

"That still doesn't give you the right to sneak out in the middle of the night!"

Dad continued to read the editorials and letters to the editor from yesterday's paper. He always said they were better than the comics.

"And to think you were actually downtown in the thick of it. You could have been arrested yourselves, or you could have been caught in the crossfire!"

Dad lowered the paper. "I never knew there was any shooting."

"Well, there *could* have been. The way I heard it from Mrs. Filbert, things were pretty tense down there. The boy reached into his pocket and, well, the whole street almost exploded into gunfire."

"It did not," I said.

"He was armed!" Mom insisted.

"All he had was a crowbar."

Ignoring this eyewitness report, Mom went on, "I heard the boy put up quite a fight."

"He did not!"

Here it was not quite seven-thirty in the morning

and Mom had already gotten all of the facts, most of them wrong. As Dad turned the newspaper page to the crossword puzzle he said, "What's a six-letter word for idle conversation? Oh, yeah, gossip."

Mom got very busy at the stove.

He went on, "I knew Russell Heck wasn't the thief."

"How?" I asked.

Dad chuckled. "I figured with so many people condemning him, they'd have to be wrong. He'd have to have at least one redeeming quality, although I don't know why you should praise a man for not being a criminal. Besides, he doesn't seem evasive enough to be a thief. He's too hotheaded."

As a consequence of Mom's missing on the prediction of Russell Heck's guilt, she not only forgave me for my night on the town, but also did not object, at least not too much, when I asked, "Can I go over to Chigger's house?"

"Maybe you should give it a rest," Mom suggested.

"But she and her mom are leaving Roscoe. For good!"

"Leaving?" Dad asked. "Why?"

I had promised Chigger not to tell anyone about her father's threats, so I just shrugged and said, "Partly because nobody likes her."

"Who wouldn't like her? That girl's as sweet as can be," Dad asked.

"It's mostly Buzz," I said, "although Toby and Gilman are in on it, too."

Mom and Dad were looking at each other. Dad sighed, "That's a crying shame. I don't believe in interfering in other people's business, but maybe we'll have to have a talk about this, starting with the parents of those three boys."

"What about her father?" Mom asked. "The way I hear it, he's been threatening them."

"Threatening them?" Dad asked as he rose from the table. "I knew he was off his rocker, but that's the first I've heard about this." He turned to me. "Is this true, Luke? Is that man threatening Chigger and her mother?"

Even though I was breaking my promise to Chigger, I was relieved, and even felt good, to say to my father, "Yes, it is."

Suddenly, my father was angry, but in that fine and powerful way in which you just knew that you could count on him to stand up and take on the whole world, even if no one else was willing to do so. "Hasn't Mrs. Heck ever heard of a restraining order?" he asked. "You get over there this instant, Luke."

"Where are you going?" Mom asked him.

"For starters, I'm calling Sheriff Browner," Dad said. "If he can call out a posse to arrest some stupid kid who's breaking into a coin box, he can certainly provide some protection for a mother and her child. And if he won't, I sure as hell will."

I was already halfway out the door as Dad reached for the phone.

"You be careful, Luke!" Mom shouted after me, wringing her hands together.

I ran as fast as I could, not even thinking of Chigger's father, only of my dad who could do anything. He would stand up for Chigger and her mom, and try his best to help fix their lives. Suddenly I stopped cold in the pasture and stared over the distance to their apartment. I never knew people could do it so quickly. Chigger was sitting in their old station wagon, which was loaded with suitcases and cardboard boxes. Even our moves from one military base to another had required days of packing and a moving van.

"Mom lost her security deposit," Chigger explained through the side window as I sprinted up to the car. "But she wanted to leave things agreeable with the landlord."

"What about your furniture?"

"We don't have none. The apartment come furnished. I told you we have to get out of here pronto."

"My dad's calling the sheriff," I said. "They're going to look out for you. Just wait a while, Chigger."

People in Roscoe had a real nose for drama, and a crowd had had already gathered to see Chigger and her mom flee our town, mainly Mrs. Filbert and some other busybodies from the neighborhood. But I didn't know if any of them would help her, and I wondered what they would do for excitement once she had left. As the men on the liars' bench were already saying, "That girl's an event in and of herself."

"Dad says we'll help you," I told Chigger. "Believe me, if anybody can, it's my dad."

Mrs. Heck hustled down the stairs with a box of clothes, which she tossed into the backseat. Her hair messed up, like she hadn't even bothered to run a comb through it lately, she seemed so anxious, preoccupied, and terrified, that she didn't even notice me. Fumbling for her car keys, she climbed behind the wheel.

Then, at the end of the drive Russell Heck appeared. He had come up so fast it was like he'd sprouted up right out of the ground. Striding forward he said, "I warned you, Gloria, but you wouldn't listen to me. I thought you might try something like this, but you can't run away from me. Not any more."

Everybody receded like a wave at Indiana Dunes beach. I could see people slipping away, and I hoped they were going to call Sheriff Browner, and I hoped he got here fast. "You leave them alone!" shouted Mrs. Filbert, the loose skin of her neck quivering like turkey wattles, surprising me with her courage.

"Mind your own damn business, old lady!" Russell Heck shouted at her.

Why didn't Chigger's mom start the car, I wondered, and make a quick getaway? I wished I had my squirrel gun, as if it would have done any good.

At that very moment, I became convinced that there was no such thing as bravery. I thought of Dad saying, "All's fair in love and war, when it should be the other way around." I realized I had to be a hero like my father, even if I was the biggest coward on the planet, only because, like him, I happened to be there when something needed to be done.

I stepped forward, telling Russell Heck, "You get the hell away from here."

I'd hardly ever uttered a cuss word in my life. Maybe some of Chigger had rubbed off on me. Then again, maybe I was just becoming angry like my father. Despite my cowardice, maybe I was my father's son after all.

At first Russell Heck looked strangely at me, like nobody had ever dared to get in his way before. Then, that pain coming into his face with each step he took toward me, he raised his hand in which he held a short iron bar.

"You leave them alone!" I exclaimed and lunged at Russell Heck, determined to stop him, but then he hit me. I wasn't sure, but figured it was his iron bar that clipped the side of my head. Everything, starting with my fingertips, went cold, and suddenly the ground was coming up fast to meet my face. Around me I heard scuffling and voices, mostly from the audience of busybodies.

Although my mind was a blur, I grabbed hold of Russell Heck's leg. He kicked at me, but I wasn't about to let go. Even if it cost me my life, I was going to stop this man.

"Hey, you can't do that!" someone finally shouted as Russell Heck brought the iron bar down again, on my shoulder this time.

"What kind of man hits a boy!" another person hollered.

I didn't recognize either voice, but as I grappled with Russell Heck, I knew them to be friends and neighbors.

Chigger and her mom got out of their car and fearfully approached us. Mrs. Heck pleaded, "Russell, please."

Several people surged around them—and me as I lay sprawled on the ground. It was like the time I had run into the curb with my bike and been thrown into the street, and people had rushed out of every house on the block to help me.

"The sheriff's on his way!" someone shouted, and that stopped Russell Heck cold. The iron bar dropped from his hand and clattered on the asphalt driveway as he turned away.

"Leave me the hell alone! I ain't done nothin'!" he growled, his voice dwindling into a whimper as I let go of his leg and he retreated back down the driveway. Through the blur I saw Mrs. Filbert rush forward and whack him with her umbrella, which she brought with her everywhere on the off chance that it could rain at any time in any place.

I heard a siren in the distance and saw Russell Heck turn down the sidewalk, breaking into a lopsided run on his bum leg. Then I must have blacked out for a moment.

Next thing I knew, Chigger was standing over me, muttering, "Would be like you to get in the way, Luke. You just take it easy now. You ain't gonna die or nothin', leastways I hope not."

If I hadn't been so dizzy, I would have told Chigger, "See, people around here aren't all bad. They do the right thing when they see it clearly."

Several people helped me to my feet and, although I still couldn't see straight, I kept mumbling, "I'm fine." So, they sent me home down the path Chigger had worn from her house to mine. Mom met me at the door and fussed with my injuries, telling me, "You've got your father's luck all right—just a busted lip and a bump on the noggin. Still, he must have hit your head pretty hard."

She made me lie down on the sofa, and Dad was so mad I thought he was going kill Russell Heck. My dad usually took everything in stride, except when it really mattered, as in looking after his family. He tore out of the house.

Mom put a cold, wet washcloth on my head, which didn't do anything except make water run down my neck. She had Doc Phillips make a house call, but he didn't think I had a concussion or anything serious. He prescribed rest, so for the next couple of hours Mom made me lie still. She wouldn't say anything about Chigger except that Dad and Sheriff Browner were working on it, whatever that meant. She brought me my dictionary and some books. At lunch I ate like a maniac, which pleased her no end.

"Russell Heck's gone. They took him to the VA hospital in Indianapolis," she informed me once I was done eating. "Sheriff Browner caught him trying to hitchhike out of town. Your father calmed down enough to agree to drop charges against him just so long as he agrees to get treatment, and leave Chigger and her mother alone."

"What about Chigger?"

"I'm not sure. You just worry about yourself for once this summer."

"But…."

I wanted to tell Mom that I couldn't just worry about myself. I had to worry about Chigger and just about everybody else, including my animals. In order to care for myself I also had to look out for them because, like Dad said, even if we didn't understand everything about life, we were all pieces to the same puzzle.

That afternoon Mom let me swing on the front porch as long as I wasn't too active. "You'll get well in no time flat, once I get some more good home-cooked food in you," she said.

I grabbed my stomach and told her, "I been eating enough to last me until next summer. Besides, I've only got dinged in the head."

"It doesn't matter."

I glided back and forth, thinking about how those people had chased off Russell Heck, and how they had come to the rescue. Then through the clear August light I saw her, trotting along the path toward our house.

When she reached the porch steps she squinted up at me and said, "I'm glad you wasn't kilt or nothin'."

I smiled, although it made my head ache. "Me, too."

She came up onto the porch. "You wanna climb the sycamore tree?"

"I don't know if I'm up to it yet."

She snorted, "I don't know when you ever been up to it."

"Why don't we just sit here?"

"Just like an old grandpa, huh?" she kidded, as she joined me on the swing. We slid back and forth for a while, saying nothing, because I was afraid she'd tell me the worst. Then she said, "So, me and Mom we're stayin' put. At least for the time being."

I couldn't keep a big, dopey grin off my face.

"Not that it's all that perfect around here, but Mom does have a job and, well, my dad's gone, for a while anyways. I'm almost feeling a little bit safe here in this dumb ol' town. I've never felt that way before, not in my whole, entire life. 'Course I ain't finished getting even with Buzz and them guys yet."

"Isn't it about time you forgot about those dopes?"

"It's more important than ever now, since everybody knows everything about me," she said earnestly. "It's kinda creepy, you know, not being a stranger, and I'm real worried about that ol' school startin' again. But I do want to thank you."

"I didn't really do anything."

"You at least got in the way."

I shrugged. "Well, you're my friend, my best friend ever."

"Really?"

"Sure."

"Well now, don't that beat all," she said, making

those gooey eyes at me. "I really do 'preciate what you did today, Luke. And I was just kidding about you just gettin' in the way. You stood up and fought like a man. Nobody's ever stood up for Mom and me like that before. Considering what a coward you are, that must've taken a lot of guts."

As it turned out, the biggest gossip of the summer was not the appearance and departure of Chigger's father, but Albert Lee's arrest. Although people for the most part only discussed the matter in private, he had upstaged both Chigger and me, not to mention Henry and his Indianapolis 500 racecar.

Albert's being one of us did make things different—and worse. His dad made restitution to the church and the pop machine company. He only balked at paying for the broken lock on the coin box at the newsstand. He said the police department should have to pay for it since Sheriff Browner should have stopped Albert sooner. The sheriff countered that Mr. Lee should be thankful he hadn't shot his son on the spot. The *Daily Independent Gazette* just wanted the coin box repaired and threatened more front-page news about Albert's arrest. Mr. Lee paid up immediately.

Albert was given probation, which might be considered getting off lightly, but even if he remained a model citizen for the rest of his life, I knew his acts would never be forgotten in Roscoe.

Late in August we went to the swimming pool for the last time that year. Will and I made our final ice cream run of the summer, after which Mom and Dad moved inside the house to watch Perry Como on the television. I was so bored by that show I spent the evenings behind the couch reading a book with my hands over my ears.

Just after Labor Day, Chigger and I walked to school together. After a long, hard summer, most kids were glad to get back to good old Rutherford B. Hayes, but not me. Not that I was opposed to learning, but I loved the absolute freedom of those three months of vacation.

Kicking a tin can down the street, Chigger didn't say anything except, "I hope this year's different."

"You and me both," I said. "But it has to be. We saved all those chickens. We've done so much stuff together, if our new teacher asks us to write a paper about what we did on our summer vacation, I won't know where to begin."

Chigger agreed, "It'd take more than a whole book, at least."

I was a little apprehensive because Chigger still wouldn't get anywhere near a dress and her hair was still chopped off like somebody had stuck a bowl on her head and started cutting with their eyes closed. But as we walked onto the school grounds she didn't curse once and didn't appear too eager to slug anyone. Of course, we hadn't run into Buzz yet.

"I sure hope you're right that this year's gonna be different," she sighed.

"Don't worry. This year may not be any different, but we are."

She looked at me. "Like usual, you're not making a lick of sense."

I shrugged. "We *are* different. We've been growing up without hardly even knowing it."

Chigger had to think about that a while. Then she said, "You know, I do feel different, like I can do some things for myself, without making a big ruckus."

That day it was so hot that our sixth grade teacher, Mrs. Jenkins—"Jinx" to every kid at Rutherford B. Hayes Grade School—stood at the front of the room, fanning herself with the class roster, and said with even less enthusiasm than us, "Just let me get your names." Because of the heat no one showed much interest. Even Buzz and the guys sat in the back of the room in a state of shock that summer was truly over. Methodically, Jinx arranged us in alphabetical order. "Just a little housekeeping," she said, chuckling to herself.

Sluggish with the heat and sudden confinement after a summer of running wild, everyone was automatically doing as requested, and I figured it might turn into a regular year after all, when Jinx pointed to the next desk and said casually, "Edwina Heck."

We all looked at each other. I had actually forgotten that Chigger had another name. Then Buzz, who had been shooting rubber bands at Gilman in the back of the room, jumped out of his seat and crowed, "Edwina! I knew it had to be a weird name, but Edwina!"

Gilman beat his desktop like bongos. "No wonder she wouldn't 'fess up to it."

Because of his recent problems with his brother Toby kept quiet. He sure as heck had quit bragging about Albert.

Buzz sang, "Edwina! Edwina! I just met a girl named Edwina!"

Jinx just looked at the two guys; then she told Buzz to sit down.

"Edwina!" Buzz whispered across the aisle. "They ought to put *that* in the newspaper."

"Why don't you just leave her alone?" I said.

Buzz stuck out his jaw. "Who's gonna make me?"

"I already did once. Remember?"

That shut him up, at least for the moment.

"There's no fighting allowed in this school," Gilman reminded me. All the way to recess the three guys continued to clown around in the back of the room. Jinx must be hard of hearing, I thought, or lost in a world of her own.

Out on the playground, the guys gathered around, while up on the asphalt the girls were singing: "Luke and Chigger sitting in a tree, k-i-s-s-i-n-g. First comes love, then comes marriage, then comes Chigger with a baby carriage."

The other big news of the day was Pamela Young's bra and the two ever so slight bumps on her chest, which certainly didn't need to be placed under any kind of restraint. Chigger had nothing up there. I knew from when her swimsuit sagged at the pool. But here they were singing us into marriage.

"Her name's Edwina!" Buzz told the girls. "Not Chigger. It's Luke and Edwina."

"You mean Edweenie," Gilman added.

"Yeah, yeah! We'll call her Edweenie!"

Standing to the side, Toby rubbed the palms of his hands on his jeans and said, "Come on, you guys. Why don't you lay off her for once?"

I had been sure things would improve for Chigger this year, what with everything we'd been through, and our picture having appeared in the newspaper. But maybe that kind of progress only happened in books and movies. In real life it seemed things went round and round like the seasons. In fact, things seemed even worse now because, instead of fighting back, Chigger just went off by herself to the far side of the playground.

"You're just jealous of her," I told Buzz.

"Well, she started it."

"She did not. You did. Why don't you grow up, or at least start acting like a normal person?"

"If you say so," he said, and he and Gilman nearly fell over themselves laughing.

When we returned to class after recess I was ready to transfer to another school, except there weren't any other schools in Roscoe. Then Chigger raised her hand and I broke out in a sweat wondering what was going to come out of that mouth of hers this time.

Jinx looked down the roster. "Uh, Edwina?"

The guys snorted with laughter. Buzz nearly fell out of his seat.

Chigger waited for him to get control of himself. Then she slid from her seat and stood up in the aisle. Looking right at Jinx, she said, "Edwina is my given name, Mrs. Jenkins. I'll admit it 'long as I have to. But around here most everybody calls me Chigger."

"Chigger?"

"Yes, ma'am."

"Same as the bug?"

Chigger got red-faced. "Sort of, I guess. But that's okay by me. It's still a good enough name."

"Let me get this straight. You prefer to be called 'Chigger'?"

"Yes, ma'am."

"It does have a certain, uh, charm," said Jinx, pushing her glasses up the bridge of her nose. "As everyone knows I don't care for nicknames and as a general rule forbid them, but, in this case…" She glanced down at the roster, making a note in her class roster. "We'll just call you 'Chigger.'"

"Thank you," said Chigger as she dipped back into her seat like a perfect lady.

Raising his hand, Buzz asked, "What about me? I just want to make sure you got my name right. I've always been Buzz."

Jinx frowned. "But you've got a perfectly good name, Walter. Since you brought it up, let's just call you by your given name. Okay, Walter?"

At the sound of "Walter" Gilman nearly rolled out of his desk. Even Toby grinned.

"But that ain't fair! I been called Buzz since kindergarten!"

"I won't hear another word about it, Walter," Jinx said. "I already told you that I don't care for nicknames."

I was boggled, as they say in the dictionary. Maybe there was some justice in this world after all.

Then, believe it or not, Jinx asked Chigger and me, "Didn't I see your picture in the newspaper last summer?" Chigger and I blushed and squirmed. So we hadn't been completely forgotten. Jinx swelled up and said, "My, my, I've never had *famous* people in any of my classes before."

Chigger said, "I just happen to have an extra one of them pictures right here in my shirt pocket."

"You do?"

"You can have it. I've got plenty more at home. Fact is, I got practically a whole lifetime supply of 'em."

Jinx beamed, "Well, we'll just have to put it up here on the door to the room. That way we can look at it every day."

"Every day?" Buzz asked, making a face.

"Yes, Walter," said Mrs. Jenkins.

Twisting around in her seat, in the politest tone of voice, Chigger echoed the teacher, "Yes, Walter."

Folding his arms, Buzz scrunched down in his desk, muttering, "It ain't fair. Everybody's always picking on me."

We went through spelling drills that afternoon and a geography lesson on Australia during which Buzz muttered, "I could just kick myself for giving her that name!"

Beginning to feel more like himself again, Toby said, "I'll be happy to study with you, *Walter.*"

Gilman sniggered, "And I'll help him, *Walter.*"

"Some friends you guys are!"

As the bell rang that afternoon, Chigger called across the room to Buzz, "Thanks a million for giving me that name, Buzz! I mean, Walter."

They say fame is ephemeral, but our picture stayed up in that classroom all year long, and Chigger finally began to find a home in Roscoe. In fact, to this day they still talk about her. If you don't believe me, just ask any of the old men on the liars' bench.

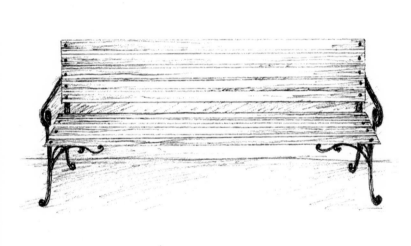

CPSIA information can be obtained at www.ICGtesting.com
Printed in the USA
LVOW050353010912

296946LV00012B/31/P